Acting Edition

Nicole Clark Is Having a Baby

by Morgan Gould

I0591014

||SAMUEL FRENCH||

FOR PRODUCTION INQUIRIES

UNITED STATES AND CANADA
info@concordtheatricals.com
1-866-979-0447

UNITED KINGDOM AND EUROPE
licensing@concordtheatricals.co.uk
020-7054-7298

Each title is subject to availability from Concord Theatricals Corp., depending upon country of performance. Please be aware that *NICOLE CLARK IS HAVING A BABY* may not be licensed by Concord Theatricals Corp. in your territory. Professional and amateur producers should contact the nearest Concord Theatricals Corp. office or licensing partner to verify availability.

No one shall make any changes in this title(s) for the purpose of production. No part of this book may be reproduced, stored in a retrieval system, scanned, uploaded, or transmitted in any form, by any means, now known or yet to be invented, including mechanical, electronic, digital, photocopying, recording, videotaping, or otherwise, without the prior written permission of the publisher. No one shall share this title(s), or any part of this title(s), through any social media or file hosting websites.

For all inquiries regarding motion picture, television, online/digital and other media rights, please contact Concord Theatricals Corp.

MUSIC AND THIRD-PARTY MATERIALS USE NOTE

Licensees are solely responsible for obtaining formal written permission from copyright owners to use copyrighted music and/or other copyrighted third-party materials (e.g., artworks, logos) in the performance of this play and are strongly cautioned to do so. If no such permission is obtained by the licensee, then the licensee must use only original music and materials that the licensee owns and controls. Licensees are solely responsible and liable for clearances of all third-party copyrighted materials, including without limitation music, and shall indemnify the copyright owners of the play(s) and their licensing agent, Concord Theatricals Corp., against any costs, expenses, losses and liabilities arising from the use of such copyrighted third-party materials by licensees. For music, please contact the appropriate music licensing authority in your territory for the rights to any incidental music.

IMPORTANT BILLING AND CREDIT REQUIREMENTS

If you have obtained performance rights to this title, please refer to your licensing agreement for important billing and credit requirements.

NICOLE CLARK IS HAVING A BABY nearly had its world premiere in the 2020 Humana Festival of New American Plays at Actors Theatre of Louisville, but was cancelled because of the Covid-19 Pandemic after only a few performances. The performance was directed by Morgan Gould, with dramaturgy by Hannah Rae Montgomery, sets by Lauren Helpern, costumes by Lex Liang, lighting design by Wen-Ling Liao, and sound design by Rodolfo Ortega. The Production Stage Manager was Kathy Preher. The cast was as follows:

NICOLE CLARK . . . . Nicole Spiezio

ROBERT ARNOLD . . . . DeShawn Harold Mitchell

HELEN CLARK . . . . Nancy Robinette

AMY RENNA . . . . Emily Kunkel

ADDITIONAL VOICEOVER . . . . Arlo Ford, Paul Werner

CHARACTERS

NICOLE CLARK – Thirties, fat, white

ROBERT ARNOLD – Thirties, Black, Nicole's Partner

HELEN CLARK – Sixties, no longer fat, white, Nicole's Mother

AMY RENNA – Thirties, Nicole's best friend from high school, thin, a townie

SETTING

Helen's house (and Nicole's childhood home) in a small town.

AUTHOR'S NOTES

I honestly don't have much to say, hopefully it's self-explanatory.

Casting

Nicole should be played by a fat actor. Sometimes people like me to define what I mean by "fat," so I will try. Fat is not just a size sixteen to eighteen. Fat is not just "I wish I could lose a few pounds." Fat is someone who is systemically discriminated against for having a larger body. Fat is a person who likely can ONLY shop at specific plus size retailers. Fat is a person who has been shamed on planes and at the doctor. Fat is a person who is NOT trying to pass as thin. This person is objectively, and hopefully proudly – or at least openly – a very fat person. This play does not make sense with someone who is not actually FAT. And hey, this actor should be easy to find, fat women don't blend in that well, try as we might!

For the story recording in the "Early Early Sunday Morning" scene, you'll need an additional male voice and a toddler voice (but just for a few moments in a sound cue!).

Saturday Morning. Early.

(**NICOLE CLARK**, *clad in matching [always] PJs, stands in her mother Helen's home in a sort of kitchen-living room combo. The kind where when the linoleum stops and the carpet begins, that's how we know we're in another room. There's a beat up mid-century kitchen table with four chairs, a Roseanne-esque couch from the eighties, beige carpeting, and maybe if we're lucky, some harvest-gold appliances.*)

(**NICOLE** *is fiddling with an ancient coffee maker, clearly a little frustrated. Desperate maybe. Is there a difference?*)

(*Nicole's mother collects Wolves. There is wolf paraphernalia everywhere. Statues, calendars, magnets on the fridge. Wolves. Everywhere. If you don't understand this, you probably grew up richer than I did. And honestly, God bless you.*)

(*The place is immaculate, though. Please don't think it isn't.* **HELEN** *would never have it any other way.*)

(*After a moment of* **NICOLE** *fiddling, in the distance we hear a song in the style of Harry*

Nilsson's 1971 hit, "Lime In The Coconut" playing. **NICOLE** *looks off.)*

(**ROBERT** *keeps singing and dance-pursuing* **NICOLE** *loudly and possibly badly humming along with the song.)*

NICOLE. I can't...this is...evil.

(**ROBERT** *keeps singing and dancing, now more louder and ridiculous than before, perhaps humping her? Up to you!)*

NICOLE. I haven't had coffee, I can't actually enjoy this –.

(**ROBERT,** *still singing, shifts tone. He starts grinding against her. It's actually kinda sexy with a pinch of goofy. He backs off throwing himself into the performance. After a moment, it turns truly sexy, sensuous. He kisses her, the music still playing – tinny and impotent – from his phone. Mid-kiss, he revs back up again at the chorus SINGING ANNOYINGLY LOUDLY AGAIN as he pulls away from her. She laughs.)*

(*She darts for his phone to turn it off, playfully. After a little moment of keep-away, he holds the phone above his head. She reaches up to get it and he kisses her again, finally relenting and giving her the phone. She shuts off the music.)*

NICOLE. MUAHAHAHAHAH [This laugh means, "I won!"]

ROBERT. No fair, I can't REALLY fight you you're WITH CHILD.

NICOLE. UGH I HATE THAT PHRASE

ROBERT. *(Sticking his stomach way out like he's pregnant.)* "I'M WITH CHILD"

NICOLE. Gross.

ROBERT. "WORSHIP ME"

NICOLE. I would never. I have never said that! Well, not since I've been pregnant –

ROBERT. "I AM THE MADONNA"

NICOLE. I barely even like children, I might not even like this one – Wait, is that how you say it though? "I am the Madonna" – or just "Madonna"?

ROBERT. I don't know, I'm not Catholic.

NICOLE. Ah, that's right, I knew you were going to hell.

ROBERT. Please, you're barely Catholic, you don't even know the Ten Commandments.

NICOLE. I know the most important one.

ROBERT. Thou shalt not tell your agnostic partner and father of your soon-to-be-child he is going to hell?

NICOLE. No, that's fine. The Bible says that's fine.

ROBERT. *(Amused.)* Uh huh, okay.

NICOLE. No, the most important one is the one about if the love of your life is pregnant and can't figure out how to use her mother's coffee pot which I SWEAR TO FUCK she got before I was even born – like we have had this one my whole life and it HAS ALWAYS SUCKED, IT'S LIKE, GOD MOM I'LL GIVE YOU THIRTY BUCKS FOR A NEW ONE SO I CAN POSSIBLY NOT WANT TO KILL MYSELF EVERY TIME I VISIT –

ROBERT. Okay, okay, relax. DEEEEEP BREATHHHHHH.

(He goes over to her and massages her shoulders. This is likely a regular thing. She calms down a little.)

Is the commandment that I should go get dressed and get you EIGHT AND ONLY EIGHT OUNCES of coffee?

NICOLE. Dunkies?

ROBERT. Well well! Aren't we fancy!

NICOLE. There's no Starbucks here.

ROBERT. STARBUCKS?! What am I, made of money?

But alas, I will do this thing you ask, but I expect compensation.

NICOLE. *(Thinking he means something sexy.)* Oh, I can do that...

ROBERT. *(Teasing, but serious.)* I meant you have to watch *Tron* with me even though you hate it. / BUT I really like that too.

NICOLE. / Ew is that the one with Spock? No!

(He playfully bites at her and then turns to head back upstairs to get ready. She grabs him. Serious for a moment.)

Hey. I love you. Thank you for putting up with this place.

ROBERT. She's not my mother. I suffer far less than you do, my love. To be honest, the worst part for me is like WHO has *a full* mattress in their guest room?

NICOLE. And why does she still put plastic underneath? I'm not five, I'm not going to wet the bed.

ROBERT. Oooooo – Maybe she thinks I will.

NICOLE. Hot.

ROBERT. Oh yeah? You like water sports?

NICOLE. Ew, actually wait no, I can't even joke about that.

ROBERT. Motherhood has CHANGED YOU!

NICOLE. HOW DARE.

> *(An alarm clock goes off in the kitchen. It's a wolf alarm clock, naturally, so it howls.* **ROBERT** *howls with it.)*

I HATE COMING HOME AHHH I HATE IT I'M SO BORED AND I HATE IT NOOOOO

ROBERT. *(Laughing a little.)* Okay, calm down, calm down it's not that bad.

NICOLE. *(Accusatory joke.)* Spoken like a man who has an incredibly healthy relationship with his mother.

ROBERT. Joyce Arnold is a saint. It's true.

NICOLE. *(A light dig.)* Guess that's where you get it from –

ROBERT. Okay, now –

NICOLE. UGH SORRY I HATE MYSELF IN THIS HOUSE IT'S WHERE FUN AND JOY AND MAGIC AND DANCING / GO TO DIE

ROBERT. Dancing?

NICOLE. *(Cleaning up her foiled coffee efforts.)* Did I tell you about the time Peter was like, "Want to hear a joke?"/ And she LITERALLY said, "I don't like jokes."

ROBERT. / Yes, I know. "I don't like jokes."

NICOLE. Who just OPENLY admits they hate LAUGHTER AND JOKES? Helen Clark, that's who. / And what about the time – I HATE WHEN YOU SAY I'M DRAMATIC – she grounded me because I brushed my hair over the sink and got hair in it. HER RULES HER RULES OPPRESS ME! // I AM ONLY ONE WOMAN I CAN'T TAKE THIS PLEASE

(**NICOLE** *starts to get nauseated [morning sickness].)*

ROBERT. / You're being dramatic.

// Alrighhhhht now you're being insane –

(**NICOLE** *dry heaves over the sink. Nothing comes. She's okay.* **ROBERT** *rubs her back She recovers.)*

NICOLE. I'm good, I'm okay.

Ugh, I can't wait for the second trimester.

ROBERT. Me neither. You'll be so cute when you're showing.

NICOLE. First, that's creepy and men shouldn't say that –

ROBERT. Why not? I'm not allowed to / like how you look?

NICOLE. And secondly, I won't show. That's like THE ONLY perk of BEING fat. You kind of always look pregnant. So when you ARE pregnant, no one notices.

ROBERT. *(Eye roll.)* Oh my god –

NICOLE. And LASTLY, I've always wanted to be like those girls on *Teen Mom* who just wear big sweatshirts and have the kid at the prom.

ROBERT. You can't be a teen mom, you're thirty-four.

NICOLE. Wow. The show is suddenly way less scary.

(**NICOLE** *puts her hand back on her stomach to settle it a little more. There's a pause.* **ROBERT** *tentatively…)*

ROBERT. You know, sometimes you could DECIDE to have a more positive attitude.

NICOLE. You could decide not to have road rage, or DECIDE to put your socks in the hamper, or not leave your toenail clippings on the bath mat –

ROBERT. Alright, jeez, alright –

NICOLE. These are all DECISIONS you could make, AND YET you do not make them.

ROBERT. You just seem a *little*...I know you do not like it when I make mood assessments /...when I assess your *moods*

NICOLE. / You are NOT in my head. Rhonda talked about this at our last appointment /...please don't make assumptions –

ROBERT. I know, I know. I'm sorry.

NICOLE. *(Practiced.)* I forgive you. I hear your apology and I believe it. And I will work towards accepting it...if

You

Would

Go

On

A

Coffee

Run

Pretty pleeeease?

> *(***ROBERT** *is deciding if he'll drop it. He does. He gently shakes his fist.)*

Thank eweeeee

> *(He exits, but he howls like a wolf as he leaves.)*

> *(Calling after him.)* I FEEL TRIGGERED BY THAT!

> *(The screen door bangs.* **AMY RENNA** *enters.)*

AMY. *(With excitement.)* FUCKING GODDAMN FUCKING CLARKKKKK AHHHHHHHHHHHHHHHHHHHHHHH

NICOLE. *(Rushing over.)* AMYYYYYYY!!!!

>(**AMY**'s *holding a drink tray filled with enormous Dunkin' Donuts iced coffee [only iced never hot, please, this is essential].* She is pregnant. Very. The two collide in an embrace, **AMY** holds the giant iced coffees outside of their hug precariously. The next part, they basically talk over each other the entire time, so please just keep talking!)

AMY. Oh my god you look / gorgeous –

NICOLE. / Wait, shut UP you glowing bitch –

AMY. *(Re: glowing bitch.)* THANK YOU / I brought DUNKIES –

>(**AMY** *hands her the coffee.*)

NICOLE. OH MY GOD THANK GOD YOU BEAUTIFUL GENIUS –

AMY. You know I gotta have my extra-extra** but wait, fuck you, you look SO / COOL THAT HAIRCUT YOU'RE SO CITY

NICOLE. STOP! You're the one we're all here for. The blessed earth mother! I hear there's a duck theme?

AMY. Haha – oh you know Deena. Always with her themes.

NICOLE. This is not as bad as your sweet sixteen where her theme was Spice Girls. / HOW STUPID

AMY. / Wait, why? I actually liked that –

NICOLE. NO of COURSE me too…me too, absolutely. I'm Scary Spice / Ahhhh

---

* A license to produce *Nicole Clark Is Having a Baby* does not include a license to publicly display any branded logos or trademarked images. Licensees must acquire rights for any logos and/or images or create their own.
** Slang for extra large coffee with extra cream and extra sugar.

AMY. / WAIT BUT LITERALLY I'm so happy you're here. I'm so fucking happy you could come eeeeeeeeeeeee

NICOLE. I would NEVER miss this. You being a mom. It's crazy. WE ARE OLD. But also? We are mature ladies of the world and it's a GOOD LOOK on us.

AMY.
GOD THE TIME
THE TIME GOES BY
SO FAST
SO EFFIN FAST
I'M TELLING YOU

NICOLE.
You're pregnant!

I'M OFFICIALLY A
SCIENCE PROJECT
And on Instagram / you
look so happy!

You aren't a science –
Everyone knows
everything on Instagram
is a lie.

AMY. Wait why? A lie why would anyone lie / on Instagram?... Like, fake news?

NICOLE. / Never mind, tell me everything! How's Tommy, how's your mom, what restaurants have changed, // and do your neighbors still have sex in their window and do you still watch –

AMY. // THEY CLOSED CHRISTOPHER'S BUT NOW IT IS A CASINO – ugh yeah but the woman has a growth of some kind –

Where's Robert?

NICOLE. Upstairs getting dressed – he thinks he has to go get coffee.

AMY. Ah, I gotcher back. My O.B. says only one cup of coffee a day but I was like HAHAHA YOU NEVER SAID WHAT SIZE

(They both laugh and grab their coffees.)

NICOLE. Okay, give me the goss, woman. Enough of this tomfoolery.

AMY. Well, I'm pregnant.

NICOLE. *(A dark joke.)* Wow. Oh my god. You want me to steal my Dad's car and take you to the clinic?

AMY. *(Playing along.)*
I'm so scared.
> *(She bursts out laughing.)*
OH MY GOD NICOLE
We can't joke about this!
It's too dark!
It's too DARK!
But also! Also!
YOU
ARE
TOO
MUCH
But also?!
I love it!
I love it!
I love it
I love it   **NICOLE.**
I love it   But wait do you love it?
Ahhhhhh

> *(They hug for a long bit.)*

AMY. Oh, Nicole, it's just been so crazy.

Honestly?

I'm not friends with Kristin anymore. I haven't spoken to her in months.

NICOLE. Whoa! What?! Whoa!

I mean, she didn't return my texts – I sent her like a birth / day text I think? I just figured she was –

AMY. / She's dating this...he lives on LIEUTENANT HAUSER...

NICOLE. Ew!

AMY. Yeah, he has like six Rottweilers and it's so gross.

NICOLE. What does Kat think of that?!

AMY. Oh, well that's the THING! That's the THING – she not at Kat's anymore!

NICOLE. OH MY GOD SHE ACTUALLY MOVED OUT OF HER MOTHER'S HOUSE I THOUGHT THAT WOULD NEVER HAPPEN

AMY. OHWAIT

JUSTOHGODWAIT

WAITFORIT

Because!

She's living with HIM!

NICOLE. OH MY GOD EW WHAT

AMY. And!

HE!

LIVES WITH HIS MOTHER TOO!!!!

NICOLE. Wait, AND the Rottweilers????

AMY. Yes! So gross!

NICOLE. So gross!

Honestly, though?

I'm not surprised – once Kat went into remission – I mean it has to be said, like, it has to be said that Kristin really put herself on the back burner. So I'm not surprised.

AMY. Yeah but you know what? She didn't even show up for LESLEY'S BABY / SHOWER

    (**NICOLE** *gasps.*)

NICOLE. Oh, fuck.

AMY. YOU KNOW HOW CLOSE THEY WERE YOU KNOW HOW CLOSE THEY WERE

NICOLE. NO I KNOW

AMY. And also! Honestly? She showed up for like THREE MINUTES to Kat's sixty-fifth, which we threw as like a big thing because of the cancer –

NICOLE. No that makes sense.

AMY. SHE ONLY CAME FOR LIKE THREE MINUTES

To her MOTHER'S cancer birthday!

Her mother whom she lived with for thirty-five years of her life 'til this weird / trashy piece of – I KNOW!

NICOLE. And the Rottweilers. Very disturbing.

    (**AMY** *hugs* **NICOLE** *tightly.*)

AMY. I LOVE WHEN YOU COME HOME!

I LOVE ITILOVE IT

How long are you staying? I don't have to do anything for the shower 'til tomorrow morning. Can we hang tonight or wait...you're probably on Helen duty...

NICOLE. Probably. I haven't seen her yet. She's been off at one of her activities since five a.m. and she was asleep when we got in.

AMY. She didn't wait up? How un-Helen!

NICOLE. Naw, that's vintage Helen. High school Helen. Now she would never stay up late to welcome her daughter and her fiancé home. Fuck no.

AMY. Is she.

Is it because.

Because...

> *(She gestures off to* **ROBERT** *– like, "Is it because Robert is Black?".)*

NICOLE.
Are you?
Are you miming blackness?
That doesn't even make sense.
And no.
She's not racist.
Well, she's tacitly racist, of
course, but she loves Robert.

AMY.

No. Now that she's not fat /   / It's *crazy* she's
anymore she's "putting herself   actually like, THIN
first."   now –

Not like me. I *ALWAYS* put
the needs of others first, cause
I'm still fat.[*]

AMY. Nooooo.

Don't say that! Noooo.

Noooooo don't say that.

Don't say that!

Noooooooo!

No!

Oh no.

Don't say that.

---

[*]A joke about how she's a little selfish, NOT a self-deprecating joke about being fat.

AMY. You're not.

And.

Don't say that! Nooooo!

Don't say that!

Noooooooo!

FEMINISM.

No!

Oh no.

Don't say that.

NO! NO! NO! NO!

Don't.

You're not. You're not EVEN.

I mean.

No.

Don't say that about yourself.

> *(Pause.)*

NICOLE. 'Kay. THAT was a nightmare.

I'm fat. Relax. It's okay. Fat people are great.

Well, like the SMART fat people like me. You need us at parties.

AMY. OhMYGOD. You're sick.

NICOLE. ...but you will have to buy more brie. We WILL eat more than most people.

AMY. Allllright. Enough.

NICOLE. There's never enough. Never enough Brie.

AMY. Mmmm. So true. So TRUE.

NICOLE. Speaking of brie...or wait no, speaking of disgusting inedible things, wanna come to dinner tonight? I'm sure Helen's gonna wanna make something and we're leaving Sunday, so it's the only night I can hang and if you're there, maybe Helen will behave. She's obsessed with babies and stuff.

AMY. Haha, oh yeah. Remember what she said at Thanksgiving? With your cousin...the annoying one who just had the baby?

NICOLE. Oh, right, where she said literal feet from Robert and me, "Can I hold your baby? I'm never having grandchildren, so I'd like to pretend." And then we shared all we were grateful for that year!!!

(They laugh for a sec. And then...)

(Sincere.) Look at you.

I bet your mom is SO EXCITED.

AMY. The ducks! The ducks!

NICOLE. Of course!

AMY. But yeah, she can't wait. When I told her at first, she peed her pants! Literally.

Literally! I mean, she'd had two bottles of courvoisier, but it was still REALLY NICE.

NICOLE. Ah, functioning alcoholism. How charming.

AMY. I've always said that.

NICOLE. So you in for dinner? I gotta tell Helen so she can freak out about the meat. Even though we all only pretend to eat it anyway.

AMY. I love pretending to eat! Remember when I was anorexic for like a couple months in high school?

NICOLE. OH WHAT A TANGLED HISTORY WE HAVE.

AMY. You can say that again!

NICOLE. OH WHAT A TANGLED HISTORY WE HAVE

AMY. *(Laughing.)* You are so FUNNY.

    Nicole, you are so funny.

    Where do you come up with these things?

    HAHAHA

      (She pregnant so it turns into crying.)

NICOLE. Honey, honey, what's wrong. Oh god, did I break you?

      (**NICOLE** *hugs her.*)

AMY. *(Crying.)* I'm just so glad you're here.

    I can't believe you're coming to my stupid baby showerrrrrrr.

NICOLE. Aim, I wouldn't miss it!

AMY. *(Crying.)* And you're like this fancy dean at Hunter or whatever –

NICOLE. I mean I don't really know about that, but there is a nice cafeteria –

AMY. *(Crying.)* And you're soooo funnnyyyyy

    What if after the kid I'm never funny with you again?

    Like our moms!

    Will I automatically become unfunny when he comessss?

NICOLE. Oh come on, you know that's not true.

    Our moms were NEVER funny.

    They had nothing to lose.

AMY. *(Sobering up.)* You're right.

    God.

    You're always right.

NICOLE. It's a gift.

(*Pensively/a joke.*) And a curse.

AMY. (*Crying again.*) God you're so funnnnyyyyyyyyy.

(**ROBERT** *enters from upstairs, dressed.*)

ROBERT. Nicole, what did you do to this poor woman?

AMY. Robert!

(*He goes over and warmly hugs her. It's a warm greeting.*)

ROBERT. She's already got you in tears!?

AMY. TEARS OF JOY

OF JOY!

ROBERT. (*Acting "girly".*) So.

Gals.

Who is sleeping with who and who got a restraining order against their boyfriend and what did I miss?

NICOLE. Rottweilers. Lots of 'em.

(**ROBERT** *grabs a coffee and sips.*)

ROBERT. Mmm. Delicious.

Did you know they're changing the name? Like KFC and DQ. Our children will not even know WHAT they are dunking in the coffee!

NICOLE. The world is a horrible place. No one should procreate.

AMY. (*Patting her stomach.*) Too late now.

ROBERT. Mmmm.

Amy, we're thinking about breakfast – wanna join?

NICOLE. Maybe Pie in the Sky?

ROBERT. OOOOO my favoriteeeeeee.

AMY. Ugh, I wish, but I have to go get Tommy's car with him. He left it at Shucker's because he got so piss-drunk last night even HE wouldn't drive it home.

NICOLE. I hate how all of you drive drunk it's so weird and awful.

AMY. Listen, we don't have a twenty-four hour train system. Plus, we're all used to it.

NICOLE. Like ten people in our class have died in drunk driving accidents!

AMY. We graduated with like one thousand so ten isn't THAT bad.

NICOLE. Oh my god.

ROBERT. I've seen you drive high! Remember in college, that trip to Woodstock –

NICOLE. High is different, high doesn't count. / I drive like six miles per hour while high, I could hit a chipmunk and it would live – *(To* **ROBERT.***)* Traitor!

AMY. / AH HA!!!! Robert's singin' like a canary now!

> *(***ROBERT*** *tweets like a bird and flys a little. He pecks at* **NICOLE***'s shoulder, she shrugs him away.* **AMY** *gathers her things and goes in to hug* **ROBERT.***)*

Okay, weirdos, I have to go so Tommy isn't late for his shift.

> *(She goes to hug* **NICOLE.***)*

See you both tonight for pretend eating.

ROBERT. Oh, you're coming to dinner?

AMY. Yup, see you then.

> *(To* **NICOLE.***)* Love you. So glad you're home, I'll text you when I'm on my way tonight.

NICOLE. 'Kay, love you too.

> *(The screen door bangs.* **AMY** *is gone.* **ROBERT** *looks at* **NICOLE.** *She loudly and intentionally slurps her iced coffee.)*

ROBERT. *(Re: the baby.)* Did you tell her?

NICOLE. No, I don't want to take away from her weekend.

> *(***NICOLE** *takes a sip of coffee.)*

ROBERT. *(Re: the coffee.)* I don't wanna be that guy, but I don't think you should have that much –

NICOLE. WHAT DID I SAY LAST TIME WE FOUGHT ABOUT THIS.

ROBERT. Okay, okay, your body, I know.

> *(He sidles up to her sweetly.)*

It's just that it's my little eggplant in there, and I don't want her to be deformed or anything.

NICOLE. We got the blood test! We know she's not retarded.

ROBERT. I hate when you use that word.

NICOLE. Oh my god WHAT is the word.

ROBERT. You are a DEAN at a UNIVERSITY.

NICOLE. Yeah, but I'm the DEAN OF STUDENT LIFE. That's like when when nutritionists are supposedly doctors. It doesn't count. If you had a heart attack WHAT is a nutritionist gonna do about it?!

ROBERT. Now I know you don't feel that way, Madame Work-a-holic. Miss "I'm the youngest dean in history..."

> *(***NICOLE** *grins devilishly. She looooves a good compliment about her achievements.)*

NICOLE. Stopppppp. *(She means keep going.)*

ROBERT. *(Moving towards her, snuggling up.)* On our very first date, I was like

MMMMM

She is so fucking fierce

> *(He kisses her.)*

ROBERT. And smart.

> *(He kisses her again.)*

And scary!

> *(He laughs. She hits him lightly, playfully.)*

NICOLE. You mean sexy scary, right?

ROBERT. Rigggggghtttttttt

> *(She playfully slaps him again.)*

So. Amy's coming to dinner. You really need a cushion for your mom THAT bad?

NICOLE. Bad-ly.

ROBERT. *(Still with a smile in the same sweet tone.)* Wow, I really still hate when you do that.

> *(**NICOLE** sips her drink, avoiding. **ROBERT** waits her out.)*

NICOLE. I just! It's easier the more people who are here.

ROBERT. But last time you came back here you said you wanted me to stay in the city so you could "be emotionally abused in peace."

NICOLE. I can't decide which is worse!

ROBERT. I can.

> *(A pause.)*

NICOLE. It's really not fair how they don't tell you when you are in a healthy relationship the other person will make you like, emotionally grow and stuff. I just wanted you for your bod.

ROBERT. I hate the word "bod."

NICOLE. BOD

BOD

BOD

BOD

ROBERT. WITH CHILD

WITH CHILD

WITH CHILD

NICOLE. ALRIGHT FINE YOU WON THIS ROUND

(They stop. **ROBERT** *takes her hand.)*

ROBERT. Listen, you're an adult home for your best friend's baby shower.

You can just, like, DO THAT and not have it be a huge rollercoaster of bullshit, right?

And in the end, if your Mom is difficult –

NICOLE. *(Understatement of the year.)* DIFFICULT! Difficult is my literal GOAL WEIGHT!

ROBERT. *(Not letting her joke.)* Nicole, I feel like sometimes you forget this isn't like when you were a kid. You're not alone. We're a team.

NICOLE. *(She means it.)* I know. I know that.

ROBERT. And when the shower is over tomorrow, we'll wake up the next morning, have breakfast, and drive home. Back to our apartment, and the cat –

NICOLE. We don't have a cat.

ROBERT. I have made so many sacrifices for this relationship.

> (**NICOLE** *smiles.*)

See? I can be the funny one too.

NICOLE. Fat people are always supposed to be the funny one.

ROBERT. What? Fuck that, WE'RE supposed to be the funny ones! Eddie Murphy! Chris Rock! Someone...else...

NICOLE. Really? You could only name TWO black comedians? TWO? And they're both from like 1992 / HELLO – You are NOT the funny one. //

ROBERT. / THEY ARE STILL EXTREMELY HILARIOUS.

// The level-headed one?

NICOLE. Yes. You can be that one.

> (*She reaches out. He goes to her. They hug, swaying a little in the kitchen.*)

At dinner, don't forget no weird doting man shit about drinking / or beef –

ROBERT. Beef? I've never said anything about beef...and the doctor said only ONE GLASS –

NICOLE. I KNOW THAT

I KNOW THAT

Just don't do any obvious weird Dad stuff.

ROBERT. Fine.

NICOLE. When we do tell people, can we be super basic and do like a gender reveal party? Except it turns into a murder mystery party that actually turns into a murder? MUAHAHAH My mom would love that.

ROBERT. (*A joke.*) Well you did say she's a monster who doesn't like parties.

NICOLE. Ah! The funny one!

ROBERT. Told you.

> *(A pause.)*

NICOLE. Hey.

I know I'm always like, she's the worst.

But she can be maternal. She can be kind and... I mean.

This is the woman who saved up her tips from her chambermaid job for two YEARS to buy me an American Girl doll.

ROBERT. Shit. That's an expensive doll.

NICOLE. And to think. Megan Walantis had FOUR of them.

ROBERT. Gross.

NICOLE. Totally.

You know.

I *have* seen her be...like a mom, you know?

ROBERT. I've seen it too. I've definitely seen it in her.

NICOLE. Do you see it in me, too?

ROBERT. Of course I do.

NICOLE. *(Shudders.)* Wait!

I feel something –

ROBERT. A kick? / Lemme –

> *(He touches her belly.)*

NICOLE. / No! Excitement! Like, I'm kind of excited.

I have an alien inside me who is drinking my blooooood.

ROBERT. That's not. Correct.

NICOLE. I'm not a scientist.

ROBERT. It's okay I forgive you.

NICOLE. EEEEEE BEING PREGNANT IS WEIRD AND FUNNNNNN

> *(She starts dance around,* **ROBERT** *dances too, it's cute.)*

ROBERT & NICOLE. *(Like dummies, chanting like a congo line.)* Alien inside of me

Alien inside of me

ALIEN INSIDE OF ME

> *(The screen door bangs.* **HELEN** *is home.)*

HELEN. Who's inside of you?

ROBERT. Helen!

> *(He goes to give her a hug.)*

HELEN. Careful of my shoulder –

> *(He is very careful.)*

NICOLE. Your shoulder?

HELEN. Busted it in dance aerobics class. Some old BAT left her dance baton out and I slipped on it, thank GOD Lenny – you remember Lenny / – was there to catch me.

NICOLE. / No. Who's Lenny?

ROBERT. It's good to see you, Helen.

> *(**HELEN** goes over to **NICOLE** and they hug.)*

HELEN. Hi, sweetheart.

> *(She looks her over.)*

I like your hair.

NICOLE. Thank you.

HELEN. That's a flattering top.

NICOLE. Thank you.

HELEN. The color is...unique.

NICOLE. Thank you?

HELEN. Where did you get those slippers?

NICOLE. TJ's...?

HELEN. They look tight.

NICOLE. They're fine.

HELEN. You have wide feet.

NICOLE. I know that.

HELEN. I wouldn't want you to get corns.

NICOLE. How sweet.

HELEN. Is that a new color of foundation?

NICOLE. I'm not wearing makeup.

HELEN. I like the eyeshadow though.

NICOLE. Okay /

(She turns to **ROBERT.***)*

HELEN. *(Announcing.)* / I was at a rehearsal.

NICOLE. Before nine a.m.?

HELEN. The play is about women on a swim team. The director is very method, so we rehearse at the pool in the very early morning, just like they do in the play.

I think it's ridiculous.

But who am I?

I've only been in one hundred million plays.

(**HELEN** *goes to the fridge. She starts getting out things.*)

HELEN. Did you see what we have?

Eggs.

I bought two dozen, I don't know how many you eat.

NICOLE. I eat ten at a time –

HELEN. WHAT?

NICOLE. I'm kidding, Mom. I eat two. Two.

(**HELEN** *begins making breakfast.* **NICOLE** *mouths to* **ROBERT** *"Three," he laughs a little.*)

HELEN. I haven't had breakfast. Have you two had breakfast?

ROBERT. No –

(**NICOLE** *elbows him.*)

HELEN. No?

NICOLE. He means yes!

HELEN. If you're hungry, there's tons of food in the fridge.

There's lunch meat – I have roast beef, turkey breast.

I still sometimes get salami because even though it's been ten years, I honestly still forget that your father is dead and he loved it, so.

There's cheese, but I can't eat that.

It's left over from my women's group.

I told them I can't have it and not to leave it.

If you check the crisper – that's the drawer on the right I have celery but it might be limp, which honestly?

I've been doing that thing where I suspect it's limp so I'm avoiding it, but really I should just put it in a soup – I have this zero-calorie minestrone – or THROW. IT. OUT.

But I hate waste.

I hate throwing out food.

Especially with your father's old debt... I'm practically penniless.

Oh!

In the freezer there's hamburger meat, I don't know HOW you'll defrost it, but I suppose you're both adults –

NICOLE. We're. We're okay, Mom. We can look and see what's there.

HELEN. I didn't buy much for you.

It's only two days.

And I never know what you're eating.

And I used to just – I would go crazy and buy things.

But you know, without your father, money is so tight.

It's tight and I don't even know what you two eat, so I didn't go crazy.

I made a deal with myself not to obsess about it.

It's not my problem, you're both adults so you can figure out what to eat.

The other three hundred sixty-three days of the year, you obviously EAT.

> (*She glances at* **NICOLE**. **NICOLE** *begins to have a reaction.*)

ROBERT. So. The play...the swimming play? What's it about?

> (**HELEN** *begins chopping veggies. She speaks on rhythm. Chopping on each period.*)

HELEN. I am.

In.

HELEN. A.

Production.

Of.

The.

Dixie.

Swim.

Club.

ROBERT. Sounds fun!

(*Chop.*)

HELEN. (*With no affectation.*) Yes.

(*She chops a little more.* **ROBERT** *is not sure
if she's going to elaborate. He's about to ask
something else and –.*)

So my friend Joan – who honestly just thinks she knows
EVERYTHING about the theater – she is just THE
WORST sometimes, I mean I love her, but she is the
worst...she had to quit and here I am cleaning up the
pieces. I didn't even want to, I wanted a break because
its been NONSTOP since I played the charwoman in
Scrooge last year –

ROBERT. Charwomen?

HELEN. Small part, but very critical –

(*Chop.*)

NICOLE. Joan quit? That doesn't seem like her. (*To* **ROBERT.**)
She's kind of like my Aunt, they're best friends –

HELEN. (*On a chop.*) Congestive heart failure.

NICOLE. WHAT?! Joan has congestive heart failure???

HELEN. Yes, and I told her you can live with that for up to three years, sometimes five, but she quit anyway.

> *(Chop.)*

ROBERT. Wow.

HELEN. I know.

I hate quitters.

> *(Chop. Chop.)*

But I like the play.

I like my *role*.

You know, when your father was alive, I always felt so guilty doing plays –

NICOLE. You did plays constantly.

HELEN. It's so nice not to feel guilty AT ALL.

My life is mine.

> *(Chop.)*

Don't get me wrong, I adored your father, he's a saint for putting up with me, but it's nice not to worry about anyone but ME for a change.

> *(**NICOLE** opens her mouth to say something snide, **ROBERT** shushes her instantly.)*

And I can really concentrate on the role.

ROBERT. That sounds nice.

> *(**NICOLE** reaches to grab a piece of carrot or something.)*

HELEN. Do you need that?

NICOLE. Yes.

HELEN. I'm just asking. I ask myself too, you know. I always ask, "Do I NEED this food?" And the answer is OFTEN "No."

NICOLE. *(Under her breath.)* Well, I'm more of a "yes" gal –

HELEN. Ha, well, I can understand that. You have to put effort into restraining yourself. I could never do it with kids and working full-time, and your father was SUCH a bad influence on me – he was such a snacker. But now I have no excuse not to put myself first. I used to never put myself first.

> *(Chop.)*

> *(Chop.)*

> *(Chop.)*

> *(****NICOLE**** seethes.)*

Oh, Nicole, you know who is in *Dixie Swim Club* with me?

NICOLE. No.

HELEN. Sandy!

NICOLE. I have no idea who that is.

HELEN. Yes you do!

NICOLE. I do not.

HELEN. It's Bronwen's mother.

NICOLE. ...

HELEN. FROM LOCUST STREET.

NICOLE. Our neighbors when I was four?

HELEN. Yes! Yes!!!! You loved little Bronwen. You know, she's doing so well. She's gorgeous. She has a daughter. She sells insurance. She's gorgeous.

NICOLE. Mmmm.

(A pause. Awkward.)

HELEN. Also Pat McKernan is in it – you remember Pat, right Nicole?

NICOLE. No.

HELEN. Yes you do. Her husband died in his armchair and your father had to go over and –

NICOLE. Oh, the lady with the huge nose who does the costumes?

HELEN. She's also an actress, but yes. She often tries her hand at the costuming. It's community theater, we all have to wear MANY hats.

ROBERT. That sounds great.

HELEN. It's actually a lot of work.

ROBERT. Yes...that too, of course!

HELEN. I'm the props mistress.

I have to keep all the props organized. People just come in and just throw things around. Part of the problem I always tell Mitchell is that we CANNOT act like people at the strike parties are going to really INVEST in the space.

(Chop.)

We have to set aside DIFFERENT times to do the detail work. Organize the box office, clean the prop loft, go through costume storage.

(Chop.)

HELEN. But who am I? Only a woman who has been involved there since 1971. What do I know?

(Chop.)

I do like this role though. I was scared at first because I thought I would have to wear a swimsuit. THANK

GOD the director's concept means we're wearing robes, mostly. Except for Greta.

(She makes a "it's gross" face.)

NICOLE. Mom! Don't body shame.

HELEN. What? She's thin, I wasn't body shaming! It's just her skin hangs down. She should never be sleeveless.

*(**NICOLE** lays her head down on the table, annoyed.)*

ROBERT. What, um...so the role is good?

HELEN. Yes. I wish I had more funny lines... I think I would be better in the larger, funnier role, but I'm also the oldest, so they had to make me the oldest part, which...well, I die in the end –

NICOLE. *(To **ROBERT**.)* Spoiler alert.

HELEN. – so I'm not in the last scene. But I like her.

I'm LEARNING to like her.

I was YouTubing other productions – Nicole! I can YouTube now –

NICOLE. *(Unenthused.)* Great.

HELEN. YouTubing, you know, to see how people said the lines, what they did.

Honestly, I like my interpretation better than any of the productions I saw online.

Even the professional ones.

Interpretation is my strong suit.

ROBERT. That seems important.

HELEN. Oh it is.

(Chopchopchop.)

The other women in the cast. Their interpretations are not as good, you know.

ROBERT. *(Sympathetic.)* Are the other women not so good?

HELEN. Three fifths of us are.

ROBERT. Two fifths are bad? That seems like a lot –

HELEN. Well, I'm good, Pat McKernan is good (Though she mugs when she has to cry), and Vivian Braithwaite is AMAZING – we always go up for the same roles – she has a better singing voice, so people are VERY taken in by that –

NICOLE. Well, you guys mostly DO musicals –

HELEN. But Joanna Stephens and Annie Hart Cool are ABYSMAL actresses. Your father – EVEN YOUR FATHER – used to say if you put them in a paper bag they COULD NOT act their way out of it! Honestly, I'd be mortified!

ROBERT.	**NICOLE.**
Abysmal?	Mom! Those are LITERALLY my godmothers.

HELEN. I'm just being honest.

NICOLE. *(Heating up.)* No, that's actually being mean.

HELEN. You are SO SENSITIVE. They're not HERE. They can't HEAR me.

NICOLE. It's supposed to be FUN. Some people just do it for FUN.

HELEN. Right, that's why they're / abysmal!

ROBERT. / What's for dinner? I could take us out –

HELEN. I can't go out it's Friday.

ROBERT. Oh...

NICOLE. Tomorrow is weigh-in day.

At weight watchers.

HELEN. I can only eat fish tonight. Fish and veggies. Have you seen this stuff?

> *(She goes to the fridge and takes out a container of Olivio.* She shows it to **ROBERT**.)*

HELEN. ZERO CALORIE BUTTER SPRAY. And it doesn't taste like chemicals. Here, try it!

ROBERT. No, thanks, I'm okay –

HELEN. Just one spray –

ROBERT. It's ten a.m. –

HELEN. You'll love it –

> *(She sprays it in his mouth. It's obviously disgusting.)*

ROBERT. MMMMMMMMMMM.

> *(**NICOLE** looks at him, a little smug.)*

HELEN. I just spray that on everything. It's like I'm not even on a diet.

Did I tell you both there's roast beef? Does anyone want any?

NICOLE. We haven't even had breakfast.

HELEN. I thought you said you had!

I have Arnold's sandwich thins. I have lettuce.

But honestly, I decided NOT to go crazy this time, I didn't get anything I couldn't have.

---

* A license to produce *Nicole Clark Is Having a Baby* does not include a license to publicly display any branded logos or trademarked images. Licensees must acquire rights for any logos and/or images or create their own.

There are the prepackaged hard-boiled eggs. I know they are an extravagance but I just hate boiling them every week.

I tell myself I've earned it. I've earned a luxury item.

> *(To* **NICOLE**, *pleasantly.)*

You know your father's medical bills mean I have absolutely no savings, right?

NICOLE. *(A snarky aside to* **ROBERT** *that* **HELEN** *doesn't clock.)* Well, he did die eleven years ago, so maybe she spent it on hard-boiled –

ROBERT. *(Clearing his throat.)* So. Tonight...I thought we could go somewhere special, my treat, ha, we can order fish –

HELEN. I already got out the meat.

ROBERT. I'm sorry?

HELEN. The meat! It's already out – not for me, god no, not on the night before weigh in, but I got out pork tenderloin from the garage freezer –

ROBERT. Oh, that sounds...great.

HELEN. I mean you don't have to have it. The meat. You don't have to have the meat if you don't want it.

ROBERT. No, that's fine –

HELEN. It's just, Nicole told me you'd both be here... I meal plan, I PLAN things, so I got it out. And it costs a lot, the meat.

ROBERT. Sure, great, well, I love meat.

HELEN. No need to placate me. If you don't want it, it's no big deal.

Nicole always used to do this in high school.

She was so inconsiderate. I would get out the meat...
I would even ask two, three, four, five, six times a day
ARE YOU GONNA BE HOME FOR DINNER and she
would say yes so I'd get the meat out and then I'd see
her pull in the driveway with her friends and they'd all
have McDonald's cups. She would throw it in the trash
by the curb, but I would see.

NICOLE. Gee, I wonder why I felt smothered by you?

HELEN. I never smothered you! I gave you independence!
I never asked you a THING about your personal life.

NICOLE. *(A joke for Robert's benefit.)* You still don't.

HELEN. That's right! Be grateful. My mother read my
diary. Very invasive.

NICOLE. I never had a diary.

ROBERT. *(A joke to lighten.)* And look at you now, you
turned out okay.

   (To **HELEN.***)* Did you hear, Nicole is officially the Dean of –

HELEN. You'll have the pork and I'll have the bluefish.

   Nobody likes bluefish but me.

NICOLE. Amy is coming too.

HELEN. Amy! How's her Mom? What is the theme of
the shower –

   BUT WAIT CAN PREGNANT WOMEN HAVE PORK
   OR IS IT JUST SALMON THEY CAN'T HAVE

   God, it's been so long and I'll never have any
   grandchildren so who can say?

NICOLE. She can eat anything, Mom.

HELEN. I don't know if I got out enough meat! / She's tiny
though, she obviously doesn't eat much –

NICOLE. / Mom, there's plenty of meat, it's fine.

HELEN. *(Bustling offstage to the garage.)* I could take out another tenderloin but that's expensive and I'm not sure it'll be defrosted in time and I can never predict the microwave timing for DEFROST, you know –

(She's gone into the garage. Still talking.)

NICOLE. *(To* **ROBERT**.*)* So like.

Are you wicked excited for the meat?

ROBERT. You're the worst.

(The screen door bangs.)

HELEN. There isn't another tenderloin so we will have to make due. I'll make extra baked potatoes. Nicole doesn't like them but everyone else in the world does so I'll make three and you can have two since you're a man and Amy can have one because she's so skinny! She probably only wants one even though she's EATING FOR TWO. I promised myself this visit I would NOT drive myself crazy about the food. I would NOT worry about what you all ate because...honestly, I just. Now that I'm officially a senior citizen, I'm taking back my time!

ROBERT. I think that's great.

HELEN. SHOOT

SHOOT

SHIT!

ROBERT. Are you okay?

NICOLE. What?

HELEN. OH GOD OH GOD SHOOT SHOOOOOOT

NICOLE. Mom? What's wrong?

HELEN. It's eleven! I AM LATE FOR SWIM CLASS, I HAVE TO CHANGE.

> (**HELEN** *starts frantically eating the veggies she's chopped but also running around the kitchen gathering things, but not really logically.*)

NICOLE. Didn't you just come from the pool?

HELEN. That's different, that's...I can't explain it – I CAN GET FLEX POINTS FROM DOING IT. I don't lose weight from standing in the pool saying lines!

> (*She runs off.*)

ROBERT. Flex points?

NICOLE. I'll explain later.

ROBERT. ...I'm scared.

NICOLE. That's valid.

> (**HELEN** *returns holding her suit and pool bag. She stuffs more veggies in her mouth. She starts switching stuff from her purse to her pool bag.*)

ROBERT. Well, have fun?

HELEN. Nicole, check on the meat. Flip it over if you need. It's in the garage.

NICOLE. Okay.

HELEN. There's food in the fridge.

Roast beef.

Some cheese.

There's even salami.

I have salad stuff too.

But I didn't want to, you know,

> (*She hunts in her purse.*)

...go crazy.

Oh! There's carrots.

> *(She finds her wallet in the depths of her purse, throws it into her pool bag. She stands, about to exit.)*

I'll be back around lunch time. We can make something.

ROBERT. Sounds great.

HELEN. What will you do while I'm gone? Will you be okay? I have wireless! I know the password is somewhere –

> *(She starts digging around the kitchen for it.)*

NICOLE. Oh, don't worry about us.

ROBERT. We'll just like, hang out.

NICOLE. We're fine.

ROBERT. We'll like...swing on the porch swing, you know. We're all good.

> *(**HELEN** stops digging. There's weird silence. **HELEN**'s "Exiting" energy dissipates.)*

HELEN. The porch swing?

ROBERT. Sure! Why not? We're in the country! When in Rome!

> *(Another silence.)*

HELEN. Hm.

ROBERT. Is that?

I mean, we don't have to swing on the swing...?

HELEN. Yes, I'm not sure if I feel comfortable with that.

ROBERT. Oh. Okay.

> *(Awkward silence. **ROBERT** looks towards **NICOLE**. She is looking away. No help.)*

HELEN. It's just. It was a very expensive swing. I've had it for a long time.

> *(Another silence.* **NICOLE** *knows where this is going. She knows exactly.)*

ROBERT. *(Not understanding...Ah what bliss not to understand!)* Okay. Well no problem. We will. Sit somewhere else.

HELEN. I'm grateful.

It's just very old.

ROBERT. Sure.

Sure thing.

> *(There's a pause.)*

I mean, we would have been care / ful...?

NICOLE. / She's saying I'm too fat for the swing.

ROBERT. What? Nicole! No she's not.

> **(HELEN** *says nothing.)*

NICOLE. We won't sit on it.

HELEN. It cost a lot.

ROBERT. Helen –

NICOLE. Fine. We. Won't sit on it.

HELEN. I'm not trying to be mean. I'm just / being honest.

NICOLE. / No, you're just being honest.

I know. It doesn't matter that I've sat on it before. For years. You have to be honest about it NOW.

HELEN. You're bigger than you've ever been before –

ROBERT. Helen! Whoa now –

NICOLE. *Robert.*

ROBERT. *(Pleading.)* Honey... I can't just.

NICOLE. I'm. Fine.

HELEN. I just get worried about that swing.

NICOLE. The swing. Of course.

HELEN. And, you know. It's not meant to bear so much...weight.

>   *(Silence.)*

I didn't sit on it when I was your size / either.

NICOLE. / I won't sit on the *fucking* swing.

HELEN. Well, you don't have to use that kind of language.

>   *(Silence.)*

ROBERT. Helen.

I'm sure you didn't mean it like it sounded.

I have to believe you didn't mean this like it sounded.

HELEN. I did actually.

I did mean it like that.

>   *(Another silence.)*

I have to get to swim class.

>   *(Another silence. **NICOLE** might be holding back tears, perhaps. But no matter what she will not look at **HELEN**. **HELEN** grabs her bag.)*

>   *(She exits.)*

>   *(The screen door bangs.)*

>   *(A moment.)*

>   *(**HELEN** doubles back, grabs a giant pool noodle.)*

(The screen door bangs again. She's gone.)

*(**NICOLE** is quiet for a moment. **ROBERT** sits next to her.)*

ROBERT. Hey. Look at me.

Look at me.

ROBERT. Listen when I very sincerely tell you.

You are beautiful to me at any size.

NICOLE. Okay.

ROBERT. What?

NICOLE. I actually am not sitting here thinking "I hope Robert thinks I'm beautiful" – that is actually not what I'm *concerned with* right now.

ROBERT. Okay...

NICOLE. Being BEAUTIFUL does not change the fact that I can't ever seem to remember why I come back here.

Being BEAUTIFUL does not make it clear why I continue to come back to this woman who treats me...

But thank you, Robert. I'm so glad you think I'm BEAUTIFUL.

ROBERT. Listen. I'm trying here.

I'm trying my best, Nicole.

NICOLE. You're doing a BEAUTIFUL job.

ROBERT. *(Taking a breath.)* Okay.

I am trying to have empathy here.

I can see you're hurt and weaponizing / sarcasm against me –

NICOLE. / Please try to sound a little less like a self-help book, it's exhausting.

ROBERT. God, I can never do anything right with you! Every time we come here, I try to say and do everything perfectly –

NICOLE. I know. I can tell. And I feel like you *do* do everything right and it's designed to make me look like some unreasonable monster!

ROBERT. You said it not me.

NICOLE. OKAY FINE THANK YOU ROBERT

Thank you for telling me you find me beautiful!

That is the ONLY thing I care about – you thinking I am attractive so that you will desire to put yourself INSIDE ME

ROBERT. Don't be like that – don't make this harder than it already is –

NICOLE. I DON'T SEE HOW SOMETHING COULD POSSIBLY BE HARDER FOR ME THAN THIS IS

ROBERT.

You think this is hard
FOR YOU?
I'm losing my fucking
SHIT!
I HAD TO LISTEN TO
HER SAY THAT SHIT
TO YOU
AND I HAD TO BE
POLITE!
So please don't take this
out on me!   **NICOLE**.
God, every girl I've ever   Actually you didn't have
dated has this shit with   to be polite –
her mom! It's so boring!
Some people have real
problems! Some people
actually struggle.

NICOLE. Oh, like you?

ROBERT. I didn't say that.

NICOLE. Whatever. I know you think that. But you have like six degrees and you went to an Ivy League school and you look like a fucking model. You're fine.

ROBERT. I KNOW THAT I NEVER SAID I WASN'T AND YOU ARE FINE TOO.

NICOLE. I NEVER SAID I WASN'T I ACTUALLY DIDN'T SAY ANYTHING

(Fake dialing a phone.) BEEP BEEP BEEP HI RHONDA SOMEONE IS MAKING ASSUMPTIONS AGAIN

ROBERT. GOD, BEING FAT IS NOT A DISABILITY.

NICOLE. I KNOW I TRIED TO SAY IT WAS ON MY COLLEGE APPS BUT IT DIDN'T WORK. THAT'S WHY I DIDN'T GET A SCHOLARSHIP AND ONLY WENT TO A STATE SCHOOL. WHO IS OPPRESSED NOW?

ROBERT. Nicole, I'm so sick of this shit, I'm sorry I called you BEAUTIFUL. What a horrible person I am! I'm sorry you're so fucked up you can't just take COMFORT from me.

NICOLE. Nothing about saying that is comforting!

ROBERT. ENLIGHTEN ME, PLEASE!

NICOLE. I don't want to be beautiful. I don't care about being beautiful. Also thin people are so stupid. You think I'm just like groveling like, "Oh you're so hot! Thank god you wanna fuck me!" Sometimes I don't wanna fucking fuck YOU! I'm not just GRATEFUL all the time –

ROBERT. I never said I thought you should be –

NICOLE. I DON'T HAVE VALUE JUST BECAUSE I AM, IN YOUR VIEW, BEAUTIFUL. I HAVE VALUE BECAUSE I'M A HUMAN BEING –

ROBERT. I know that you don't have to tell ME that!

NICOLE. – and my GOD if we have a girl you better get this right with her or –

ROBERT. *(Yelling.)* OR. WHAT?

OH MY GOD

You think your Mom is tough?

She seems like a goddamn *walk in the park* to me.

She just seems like a little old bitty who likes dicing shit!

YOU?!

You're fucking SCARY.

> *(There's a silence between them.* **NICOLE** *heard that. She really did.)*

NICOLE. *(Quietly.)* I know. I'm sorry.

You're right.

> *(Pause.)*

What if I keep doing this and doing this and doing this and I can never stop? What if I don't know how? What if she ruined me?

ROBERT. *(A promise.)* She didn't.

> *(**ROBERT** takes her hand. He gives her a kiss. They sit like that for a moment.)*

Saturday Night

(**ROBERT**, **AMY**, **NICOLE**, *and* **HELEN** *are sitting at dinner.* **HELEN** *is eating her fish, of course. The rest are eating the pork. Thankfully, it defrosted in time. Thankfully.*)

(**NICOLE** *is silent.*)

HELEN. Then, you know, after that.

Well, I use the egg whites in a carton – just the generic brand.

I'm not MADE of money, after all.

I use just two tablespoons of that.

I use olive spray on the pan, that's essentially no calories at all – the spray, though, ACTUAL olive oil would put ME wayyyyy over the daily goal.

I use the frozen veggies now, I used to use fresh but it's just me, so the frozen lasts longer and is cheaper.

Then I don't feel as guilty about the pre-packaged hard-boiled eggs I eat for lunch.

HAHA

Amy, you and the baby need more pork.

(*She spoons way too much on Amy's plate.*)

So I use frozen spinach.

Then I wait a bit –

Well, salt and pepper THEN I wait a bit.

I go answer an email or two.

Then I add the no-points salsa. There's a certain brand.

NEVER USE NEWMAN'S OWN I LOVE HIM BUT
IT IS FULL OF SUGAR

So after the emails, I add the frozen onions and
peppers mix.

I stir that around a bit and add the two tablespoons of
egg whites and the salsa.

And I cover it.

Have to cover it.

While I cover it, I get the frozen fruit out –

But here's the trick, because I just leave it in the fridge,
then it's defrosted, but I don't have to worry it'll go bad.
I mix that in a little bowl with the plain yogurt – no
vanilla or flavoring – the greek yogurt NOT full milk,
that's too much...

The plain, zero milkfat NO FLAVOR.

With the frozen, well, refrigerated, fruit.

> *(She puts a bunch more pork on Robert's
> plate without mentioning it.)*

By then the omelette – egg white omelette is done –
spinach, onions, peppers, egg whites, salsa.

AND IT IS HUGE.

IT'S HUGE.

I have to eat a lot, I just eat VERY high protein.

But I do eat a lot.

I eat plenty.

I have to.

I have never been good at deprevation! Hahah!

So I have to eat a lot, but this is great because it's SO
FILLING but barely any points.

(There's a long pause.)

ROBERT. So, Amy, what were you saying?

AMY. Oh, just that this is really great, Helen.

HELEN. Thank you! I love pork tenderloin. I wish I could have some.

AMY. Oh...do you want some of mine?

HELEN. *(Looking so longingly.)* Oh, no, absolutely not.

AMY. I'd happily share.

HELEN. Haha! No! You're too thin! You need it! The baby needs it.

ROBERT. I have extra too.

HELEN. No. I love bluefish.

I LOVE IT.

Hahaha.

I mean I've learned to love it.

ROBERT. Amy, how. Is. Tommy. He must be so excited.

AMY. He is. He's already buying little mini footballs –

HELEN. I don't like football.

ROBERT. ...Okay.

AMY. And he's still at the restaurant. He's manager now, though, so. He likes his crew.

They're fun guys.

HELEN. At Quick's Hole?

AMY. Yup.

HELEN. I love that place.

So fattening but I love it.

I used to make a chicken with grapes that was a lot like their chicken, but of COURSE cheaper – it's very overpriced there.

I made it with thyme and grapes, baked, though, which sounds gross but if you think of it, it's like goat cheese and craisins, but WAY less calories.

ROBERT. You put goat cheese and craisins on chicken?

HELEN. OH GOD YES. It used to be Nicole's favorite growing up. She wanted it for every birthday.

I had to hide it in the back of the fridge from her!

Hahaha

She still found it...

She always found it.

She's smart.

AMY. *(Trying to change the subject.)* Are you in any plays now Helen?

HELEN. Yes. I'm in *Dixie Swim Club* downtown at the Players' Theatre.

AMY. Oooo fancy.

HELEN. Yes.

I wish I had more funny lines.

I think I would be better in the larger, funnier role, but I'm also the oldest, so they had to make me the oldest part.

AMY. Well you're looking so great, they'll have to put you in old-age makeup.

HELEN. No they won't, I'm an old hag. But it's okay. I accept myself.

AMY. Oh. Good.

(Pause.)

AMY. Nicole, I'm so proud of your promotion. That's amazing. Helen, you must be so proud.

HELEN. Well, I didn't do it.

Oh! Amy!

I forgot!

> *(She gets up and bustles over to a closet. She gets out a bunch of yoga mats and blocks.)*

You're so sporty, I thought you might want these. For after the baby, of course.

AMY. *(Politely.)* Oh...thanks.

HELEN. I tried to take them back to the Christmas Tree Shop, but when I got them they were on clearance so the sale was final which is RIDICULOUS because I saw ones just like it, which means they were NOT the last ones ordered, and look JUST like the ones they have in stock, so you should be able to return them, they were 4.99 each and I got four, that's over twenty dollars with tax and with Nicole's father's funeral costs and his medical bills, I don't have a penny, really. So it's a real shame.

AMY. Thank you, Helen. But you sure you don't want them?

HELEN. No, the yoga mat slips on the gym floor at the rec center where I take my yoga class and the yoga blocks I actually use for the pool – we have this stair exercise we do – and they float and then I slip off them and whenever I slip off them, I have to start the stair climb again because I am RIGOROUS with myself about starting from scratch if I break the chain. And we have to get to one hundred steps, so it's a lot.

AMY. These are great, I'll totally use them, thanks so much.

HELEN.

> You are so welcome.
> Work off that baby
> weight!
> I believe in you!
> Are people ready for
> dessert?
> I was going to make
> one of my FAMOUS ice
> cream cakes –

NICOLE.

> She's still pregnant.

AMY. OH GOD I LOVE / THOSE!

HELEN. / But I don't make those anymore because I think none of us REALLY need all that sugar. None of us want that.

> *(She sort of laughs towards* **NICOLE**.*)*

ROBERT. Oh no problem, we're not sweettooths usually at home.

HELEN. Oh no?

> Well Nicole usually is. She used to have to have dessert every night.

> She would ask Ms. McKinney for an extra cookie at snack and try to sneak it under her pillow to have at night before I saw.

> I always caught her.

> Can't bullshit a bullshitter! Haha!

> Just you wait Amy, just you WAIT!

NICOLE. I was five.

HELEN. *(To* **NICOLE**.*)* I wish a little cookie sneak on you, even though I know Madame Career Focused will never have children.

ROBERT. Never say never.

HELEN. Oh, I've given up.

Alex Wilkinson was over last week and she was showing me pictures of her grandchildren and I was jealous, but you know, I can't control you. I never have. I've never been able to control you, so I stopped trying years ago.

NICOLE. *(Sarcastically.)* Right.

HELEN. Like with Nicole's weight. She goes up and down, up and down – now she's up.

Which of course, I understand. I understand that.

I understand why she's so top heavy, she got that from me.

So I understand.

I've tried everything.

But she's her own person.

Amy, I know you're having a son.

And thank god!

Because if you ever have a daughter, just know.

She'll never listen to a word you say.

Nothing you say will ever have an impact.

The sooner you realize it, the better.

AMY. *(Searching for the right thing to say.)* Oh, I'm sure it's not that simple.

ROBERT. I think it depends HOW you say it, Helen.

HELEN. Hmmm. Spoken like a man with no kids!

With child rearing nothing is simple and no kid is grateful!

But that's not why we do it, right Amy?

You'll see soon enough.

It's not why any mother does it.

We're selfless.

As a mom, you're fucked no matter what –

Excuse my language.

But you are!

If you do it perfectly, everyone is messed up, if you're a monster, everyone is messed up. You could work a full-time job like me, and then come home, cook dinner, clean the house, help with homework – I made sure they all had straight-As – Nicole is a DEAN or whatnot now...that's because I was ON HER.

I wanted her to be the BEST she could be.

I wanted her to be better than anyone.

Especially because, well, with her weight issues.

I knew she'd have to work harder.

I always had to.

It's just the way it is.

You gotta earn respect, you don't just get given it! You know?

God, Amy, it must be so nice to just BE RESPECTED!

AMY. *(Kind of offended.)* Uh...

HELEN. And Robert! You're a man, so I can't even IMAGINE how nice that is.

ROBERT. Right, well, I DON'T think we should get into oppression wars over here about that.

HELEN. That's true. That's true. *Obviously* you've had it harder than any of us.

ROBERT. I mean, I went to Princeton, I'm okay.

HELEN. See?! And I don't have a dime.

HELEN. Anyway, as a Mother, I promise no matter what you do everyone hates you.

"She's a critical bitch."

"She was too hard on me."

"She made us do chores."

I know what you and your sister say, Nicole.

But I love you no matter what, even though you barely call.

AMY. Well, she's here now.

HELEN. Yes, but I know you hate it.

ROBERT. She doesn't hate it.

HELEN. Oh, it's okay Robert, I know she does. I made my peace with that years ago. That trip you brought your friend Joel here and we had that big blowout over borrowing the car and she had to stay at your house. (*Re:* **AMY**.)

NICOLE. Joel wasn't my friend.

HELEN. Oh. Well then why did you bring him if you didn't like him?

NICOLE. He was my boyfriend.

HELEN. Joel? No – I'm talking about the brunette fellow, that muscled one.

NICOLE. Yes, I know. He was my boyfriend for six years.

HELEN. The brunette one from somewhere in Canada?

NICOLE. YES.

ROBERT. Yeah, your college boyfriend.

AMY. Joel was sweet, I liked him.

HELEN. That was your boyfriend? Hm.

　　　　(**HELEN** *eats.*)

NICOLE. Yes. I know it's shocking. I have boyfriends. I even have hot ones.

HELEN. I know that. *(She sort of eyes* **ROBERT**, *is he hot? Sure.)*

AMY. Joel was actually.

He was very.

Haha

Joel was...

> *(She trails off. He was hot.)*

ROBERT. *(Whispering to* **NICOLE**.*)* Are you okay?

NICOLE. The fight wasn't over the car. I wanted to borrow the car to drive Joel to the bus station and you wouldn't let me borrow it. But I was driving him to the bus station because I was making him go home because he was having a miserable time because he couldn't stand the way you spoke to me and it was making him crazy and he wanted to stay but I begged him to leave because it's easier for me when you're mean to me when no one is watching.

> *(***ROBERT*** *takes* **NICOLE***'s hand.)*

HELEN. Mean to you?

NICOLE. Yes.

You are mean to me.

HELEN. I'm not mean to you!

> *(She looks at* **AMY** *and* **ROBERT** *who push food around on their plates.)*

See?

Fucked.

HELEN. Coming and going.

It's always my fault.

This is why. This is why I don't drive myself crazy anymore. Trying to please you.

Trying to get what you want in the fridge.

I shouldn't have even gotten that roast beef!

It was $8.99 a pound and I don't have a DIME now that your father –

ROBERT. HELEN!

Helen.

I'm sorry.

I have to. Put my foot DOWN.

Your daughter.

Your amazing, smart, brave, wonderful daughter is trying to talk to you.

She is trying to tell you something.

I try not to intervene.

But enough is enough.

NICOLE. Robert.

Just stop, okay?

ROBERT. *(To **NICOLE**.)* I said I'd protect you and I meant it.

*(To **HELEN**.)* I'm sorry, Helen. But.

I don't think you mean it, but you have a lot of... power...over her.

And I think you need to understand that words mean something.

Not just to Nicole.

But to me.

So this ends / now.

NICOLE. / I'm pregnant.

> *(A beat.)*

I'm having a / baby.

ROBERT.	**AMY**.
(To himself.) / Nicole.	Oh my god!

> *(Smaller beat.)*

HELEN. On purpose?

NICOLE. / Yes. God, yes. ON PURPOSE.

HELEN. Oh.

> *(There's a silence. **AMY** gets up and goes to hug **NICOLE**.)*

AMY. Nicole, congratulations. Oh my god... I can't believe it. I can't. Why didn't you tell me?! This is amazing...

NICOLE. Thank you. It's still early so.

ROBERT. Very early.

> *(**HELEN** pointedly still says nothing.)*

NICOLE. *(To **HELEN**.)* Do you have. Any questions. Like, for me...? Or, anything to say.

> *(**HELEN** is quiet.)*

ROBERT. *(Taking **NICOLE**'s hand.)* We're really excited.

AMY. I'm really excited too. Helen, we could plan a baby shower! / We can pick a theme! Scary Spice!

NICOLE. *(Like a dare.)* / Are you excited, Mom?

> *(A silence.)*

NICOLE. Are you?

> *(Another silence.)*

ROBERT. *(Trying to lighten the mood.)* We got the blood test for chromosomal –? The kid is all clear!

> *(A small pause.)*

HELEN. That's a shame, Down Syndrome children are lovely.

AMY. Helen! What –

> (**NICOLE** *starts laughing. She's laughing and laughing and she can't stop.*)

NICOLE. *(To* **ROBERT.***)* I knew it. I knew she'd say something fucked. I was right. I've never been wrong about her. Never ever once. Never.

> (**NICOLE** *keeps laughing.*)

HELEN. I know you think you can predict every single thing going on in my head, even though I can't even predict every single thing going on in my head.

So.

What do you want me to say, Nicole?

Please.

You clearly have some DESIRED EFFECT you wanted this news to have.

Fill me in.

Do you want a ticker tape / parade?

NICOLE. / No! I want you to just be normal.

I want you to JUST CRY AND SCREAM AND BE LIKE A NORMAL MOM BUT YOU NEVER HAVE BEEN / SO I DON'T KNOW WHY I THOUGHT IT WOULD // START NOW!

ROBERT. / Nicole, let's take a breath –

NICOLE. Tell me.

Tell me now.

Why you can't be normal.

HELEN. I don't know what you want me to say.

NICOLE. The truth.

Why can't you be uncomplicatedly happy for me?

You're overjoyed for Amy. You're giving her presents and asking her about shower themes. For me? You have nothing to say.

Why? Please.

I know. But I want THEM to HEAR YOU say it.

HELEN. If you already know, then why are you asking?

NICOLE. Maybe you're right. Maybe I can't predict you as well as I think.

(HELEN looks at NICOLE a long moment.)

HELEN. I just. I think you have a lot of growing up to do before you can take care of a child. There's a lot that goes into it.

ROBERT. I think we're pretty grown up, Helen.

NICOLE. I guess my job, my stable housing, my supportive partner aren't enough?

(A pause.)

HELEN. *(To NICOLE.)* I think you should be...healthier... before...you. Have a child.

NICOLE. *(She knows.)* Healthier.

ROBERT. Healthier?

HELEN. Yes, *healthier.*

NICOLE. Thinner.

(**HELEN** *doesn't answer.*)

HELEN. You told me to be honest.

ROBERT. Helen.

That is...people of all sizes have children.

(*Pause.*)

AMY. I mean, you were...you were *big*, when...

(**AMY** *trails off. Another pause.*)

NICOLE. I take it back, Mom. I don't want honesty, I want APPROVAL. The world is PLENTY honest with me AND my weight. You? You just have to say, "Great job!"

WHY ARE YOU THE ONLY MOM WHO DIDN'T GET THE MEMO?

HELEN. I'm sorry! That's not who I AM – I can't lie –

NICOLE. That's bullshit. It's not true, everyone can lie. It is God's greatest gift. You are supposed to lie and tell me you're so excited to be a Grandmother that you can barely breathe!

HELEN. I've never done that. I've never done that for you or for Emma. It doesn't do anyone any good.

NICOLE. YES IT DOES!

It would have done me A LOT of good to think your love for me wasn't conditional – on my grades, on my weight –

HELEN. My love for you isn't CONDITIONAL on anything, but those things – being thin, getting good grades, they make you happy –

NICOLE. No. They make you happy. It took me soooo long to figure out the difference.

HELEN. Jesus! Nicole! I can't say anything! You think I'm critical – you pick apart every single thing I say.

ROBERT. Helen, Nicole...let's take a –

HELEN. I just think.

Truthfully. At your weight. I wonder.

What habits will you be passing on to this child?

Have you thought about the impact...you know, that might have.

I speak from personal experience.

> (*She looks at* **NICOLE**, *referencing her size.*)

Obviously.

ROBERT. Okay. That's enough. This is my child. This is my family. Please. Enough.

HELEN. (*To* **NICOLE**.) You say I'm controlling, but you're the one controlling MY response to this news.

> (**HELEN** *looks down at her plate superior-ly.*)

> (*No one knows what to say. After a little pause...*)

(*To* **NICOLE**.) You asked for the truth.

NICOLE. (*Quiet at first.*) You are so fucking boring.

You are so fucking boring.

You are so fucking boring.

I can't hear one more thing about what's in the fridge.

STOP TALKING ABOUT FOOD. STOP TALKING ABOUT FUCKING FOOD.

You have a fucking eating disorder.

You have an eating disorder and I think you're proud of it.

NICOLE. I think you're proud you've white-knuckled yourself thin –

But at what cost?

Do you realize it is literally ALL you talk about?! You obsessively list the contents of the fridge. You listed the things in the fridge. THREE TIMES today.

Every single accomplishment, straight-A, career achievement. You have never been as happy about them as you were when I came home one summer after having MONO and I had lost fifty pounds.

You were elated. It was the only time you've ever been nice to me.

Do you know that? The only time.

It took me literal DECADES to undo what you did to me. It took me years to not hate myself the way you hate yourself. Do you remember telling me no man would ever love me because I was fat? YOU WERE FAT AND YOU WERE MARRIED FOR THIRTY YEARS UNTIL THE DAY DAD DIED.

You're a walking example that thinness doesn't buy happiness. If you took a second to just go a LITTLE DEEPER – a thing you REFUSE to do because I think on some level you *KNOW* that the thinness you've been chasing your entire life – the carrot that has ALWAYS been dangling just beyond your reach – THE MOST IMPORTANT THING YOU ALWAYS THOUGHT WOULD SOLVE EVERYTHING, didn't solve ANYTHING. THEN. You'd have to recognize that you've always been a bitter, critical, unhappy, bitch for NO reason at all. You could have stuffed your face with chips and bacon and pizza and spared yourself all the trouble.

(**HELEN** *gets up and leaves the table.* **ROBERT** *looks towards* **NICOLE.** **AMY** *does too.*)

Anyone want some more fucking pork?

> *(Maybe* **AMY** *takes some. She chews.* **NICOLE** *devours.)*

Early Early Sunday Morning

(**ROBERT** *appears from upstairs. He's holding a bunch of bags/suitcases. He tries to be absolutely silent as he tiptoes through the kitchen to the screen door with all the bags. He's almost home free, but he bangs into the corner of the counter.*)

ROBERT. *(Whispering/mouthing.)* Ow! FUCK ME

(*He continues out into the driveway. He's gone for a moment, presumably putting the bags in the car. He returns, silently heading back upstairs. We hear some muffled whispers offstage.* **ROBERT** *returns again with more bags, once again trying to silently exit without being heard. He is almost home free when his cell phone rings in his pocket. His ringtone is a loud and truly disruptive pop song.**)

(*He's holding the bags, so he can't silent it and has a frantic moment of choice. He quickly places the bags down and answers the phone.*)

(A loud whisper.) WHAT????

...

WHY ARE YOU CALLING ME FROM UPSTAIRS

...

I'm sorry. I'm not. I'm not angry.

No.

---

* A license to produce *Nicole Clark Is Having a Baby* does not include a performance license for any third-party or copyrighted music. Licensees should create an original composition or use music in the public domain. For further information, please see the Music and Third-Party Materials Use Note on page iii.

I'm not.

No.

...

JESUS, NICOLE... Okay, okay, I'm coming.

>   *(He abandons the bags and goes back upstairs for a moment.* **HELEN** *enters the kitchen. She waits in the darkness for a moment. Nothing.)*

>   *(She goes to the fridge. She opens it. She looks for a very long time, but her expression is inscrutable. (NO "Longing face" PLEASE!!!!) After a moment,* **ROBERT** *reappears with a blow dryer in his hand, plus a small backpack and Nicole's purse.* **HELEN** *shuts the fridge.)*

Helen...

HELEN. Packing up?

ROBERT. Yes. Um. I'm sorry if my phone woke you.

HELEN. I wasn't asleep.

ROBERT. Oh.

HELEN. You weren't going to say goodbye?

ROBERT. Oh. I have to work on Monday, so we thought we should pack up before the shower. And um. Be ready to leave straight from there. So.

HELEN. The baby shower isn't 'til two.

ROBERT. That's right.

HELEN. It's five a.m.

>   *(Pause.)*

ROBERT. Helen. Dinner / was –

HELEN. *(Interrupting him.)* / This is how she's always been. Hold it in, silently punish, then explode. Since day one.

ROBERT. That's not my experience.

> *(Pause.)*

HELEN. I *am* happy for her. For both of you.

ROBERT. Ummmmm

I think maybe that didn't come across tonight.

HELEN. Well she wouldn't let me get a word in.

ROBERT. Look, I really don't want to get in the middle of this with you two. My job is just to support Nicole, and I respect you, Helen, but at the end of the day, I'm just trying to build a life with my family. I'm not an expert at navigating these things.

HELEN. Ah yes, I've heard your mother is a dream, apparently.

ROBERT. We fight. We make up. It's not complicated.

HELEN. Why does everyone think I'm so complicated? I feel so simple to myself.

ROBERT. I don't think it feels simple to Nicole.

HELEN. I just want her to be happy and I want to be happy.

But it's too late for me.

ROBERT. I don't believe that, and I don't think you do either.

> *(Pause.)*

HELEN. Do you want some roast beef?

> *(He doesn't. But. Like.)*

ROBERT. Sure.

> *(**HELEN** goes to the fridge. She gets some out and puts it on the counter. **ROBERT** and **HELEN** lean, eating from the package.)*

This is good for $8.99.

HELEN. I know! I love it! I always go to Windfall for my meat, not Hannaford's or Shaw's or GOD FORBID Stop & Shop.

I also think this is organic, but it's still only $8.99.

Normally I can't afford organic, so –

(She realizes she's gone on. She chews. He chews.)

Tell me about the baby.

ROBERT. Oh. Of course. Yeah.

Well, it's – just about twelve weeks. Our little plum.

Can't wait 'til we've got a watermelon on our hands.

HELEN. You know, I remember from when I was pregnant.

THE ONLY perk of BEING fat. You always look pregnant. So when you ARE pregnant, no one notices.

ROBERT. ...I've heard that.

*(**NICOLE** enters, but **ROBERT** and **HELEN** don't notice. She listens at the door.)*

HELEN. Twelve weeks. You hoping for a boy?

ROBERT. Hm. I mean I just want a healthy child. That's all.

HELEN. Oh come on.

ROBERT. *(Grinning.)* Actually? I sort of want a girl.

HELEN. God help you.

ROBERT. God help us either way.

HELEN. Girls are the worst. They play mind games. They'll hate you.

ROBERT. I'm prepared. Bring it on.

HELEN. Call me in sixteen years. Or thirty-four.

ROBERT. Nicole doesn't hate you.

She wouldn't have come here if she hated you. I know her. She doesn't do anything she doesn't want to do. BELIEVE me.

HELEN. She only ever comes here because of guilt.

ROBERT. She's here because she WANTS to have a good relationship with you.

HELEN. We used to have one, I think. I can't remember why we don't anymore.

(**NICOLE** *covers her mouth. She might cry. She doesn't make a sound.*)

ROBERT. I think that maybe you could start by asking her questions about her. You could start like this. *(He gestures to himself and* **HELEN.***)*

HELEN. When I ask her questions she thinks I'm being critical.

ROBERT. Are you being critical when you ask her questions?

HELEN. Yes.

ROBERT. So maybe...start with actually asking.

HELEN. Hm.

ROBERT. You could keep practicing on me.

(**HELEN** *chews. After a moment.*)

HELEN. How has the pregnancy been?

ROBERT. Lots of morning sickness.

HELEN. I had that too.

ROBERT. She has trouble sleeping, acid reflux.

HELEN. She shouldn't have any caffeine.

(Pause.)

Do you have a nursery?

ROBERT. Not yet. Tiny apartment – it'll be more like "a corner." But, she's a city baby, so we'll make do. And we'll have a tiny Mets fan.

HELEN. I hate sports. I hate games, too.

ROBERT. Okay.

>   *(Pause.)*

HELEN. Names?

ROBERT. We're working on a list.

>   (**HELEN** *pauses for a moment.*)

HELEN. Ha.

>   You must think I'm nuts, huh?

ROBERT. I don't.

HELEN. She's not perfect either. She was no easy task.

ROBERT. Oh, I know.

HELEN. I bet you do.

>   You remind me of her father. He was so patient.

ROBERT. I wish I could have met him.

HELEN. Hm.

>   *(A pause.)*

>   Do you.

>   Do you need any money?

HELEN. I do have *some.*

>   I *could* help.

ROBERT. No. We're okay.

>   That's really nice of you. We're okay.

>   I mean, you know.

ROBERT. Everything is scary all the time.

But. I think we're as okay as anyone.

HELEN. Must be nice.

ROBERT. I guess it is.

> (*A pause.* **HELEN** *eats another piece of roast beef.*)

HELEN. I'm sure she won't speak to me before you leave.

She's very punishing, you know.

But I have something I want her to have.

Can I give it to you?

ROBERT. Of course.

HELEN. Stay here. Please don't go.

ROBERT. I'll wait.

> (**HELEN** *exits to her bedroom. After a moment,*
> *to* **NICOLE***:*)

Are you REALLY not going to say goodbye?

> (**NICOLE** *creeps out from around the corner.*)

NICOLE. How did you know I was there?

ROBERT. You're not like, a highly-trained operative. I HEARD YOU.

NICOLE. Oh.

ROBERT. Nicole, I think she's trying.

NICOLE. I knew you'd side with her.

ROBERT. I'm not! I'm siding with YOU. Siding with her IS siding with you!

NICOLE. I know you think I'm like, making a huge deal out of this –

ROBERT. No, actually. I don't.

I think you are making exactly the size deal out of this that you should.

I'm the one packing the bags, after all.

I guess I thought I could save you, or something. I know it's stupid.

NICOLE. It's not stupid. It's sweet.

But misguided.

You don't get it. You aren't a daughter.

ROBERT. No. But I might have one.

And I cannot deal with you catapulting into some weird abusive trauma victim state every single time we visit your mom.

NICOLE. Let's just never visit her again.

ROBERT. You say that like it's an option.

NICOLE. It is.

ROBERT. It isn't or you ALREADY wouldn't be in touch.

You want this to work, I know you do.

And now I do too. Because I care about you.

NICOLE. I've been trying to make it work for more than three decades!

What if we DO have a daughter?

I'm not going to let her do what she did to me to her.

I'm not letting her teach her that she can only love herself if she's thin.

That otherwise she has to be better than everyone and earn love through being the best.

NICOLE. I finally, finally don't believe that. It took me years to realize my perfectionism and achievement was the most insufferable thing ABOUT ME.

NOT MY FUCKING WEIGHT.

ROBERT. I can think of a few other REALLY insufferable things.

NICOLE. I have a man who loves me no matter what. He even loves me BECAUSE of who I am. AND because apparently, I am BEAUTIFUL

> (**NICOLE** *riff-sings in the style of Christina Aguilera.**)

ROBERT. Oh god help me not this again YOU ARE UGLY, I PROMISE

NICOLE. *(Smiling.)* I have a career and friends.

I have generosity and love in my life.

Why do I need this?

Why do I care about this woman who makes me feel like shit about myself?

ROBERT. Because she's your mom.

NICOLE. Not if I choose not to be her daughter.

ROBERT. You're so funny.

NICOLE. Why?

ROBERT. You're so like outspoken and fat-positive and you're SO PROUD of how you refuse to have shame about it.

But you're so bad at accepting that your mom isn't as good as you are at it.

You say you want to empower fat women, but you don't include your mom.

You say she held you back, made you feel bad.

But think about how much self-hate she has.

You'd feel empathy for ANYONE else who had that.

But you can't find it for her.

You see a woman with alllll this power over you.

And even though she says awful things?

I see a lonely old lady who only eats veggies and fish.

She probably just wishes her daughter would hug her.

NICOLE. But see, that's not fair!

How come I have to be the one to do it?

She's the mom, I'M THE KID!

She should have to hug ME!

ROBERT. You're not a child.

NICOLE. But I am! I'm her child.

And you heard her – the way she.

Why should I forgive her?

She's the one who messed up!

I didn't do anything wrong!

This is how it happens every time!

Why should I fix it?

Why should I???

ROBERT. Because maybe she can't.

And because I want my daughter to have TWO grandmothers.

ROBERT. I want you, the love of my life to be HAPPY and not crying at all major holidays because you and your mom aren't speaking.

ALSO MY GOD I JUST DON'T FEEL THAT BAD FOR YOU, YOU OWN TWO MACBOOK PROS

NICOLE. ONE IS FOR WORK

ROBERT. YOU USE THEM INDISCRIMINATELY

NICOLE. DON'T TELL MY BOSS

ROBERT. I WILL IF YOU DON'T MAKE UP WITH YOUR MOM SO WE CAN GO HOME AND LIVE IN PEACE AND NOT SNEAK OUT OF HERE AT FIVE IN THE MORNING.

(**HELEN** *renters.*)

HELEN. It's almost six now, actually.

Good morning, Nicole.

NICOLE. Morning.

HELEN. No silent treatment? You've lost your touch.

NICOLE. The hormones have weakened me.

(*There's a long silence.*)

HELEN. I am sorry.

If my honesty last night upset you.

I just.

Felt it was my duty as a Grandmother to say something.

I do care.

And I wouldn't have been able to forgive myself if I just stayed silent.

NICOLE. You weighed over three hundred pounds my entire life. And I'm just fine.

HELEN. But you're not fine.

NICOLE. There you have it!

I AM fine.

I'm fat.

But I'm actually fine.

That's where you've always, always misunderstood me.

HELEN. You know what I mean.

Life as a...large person. Nicole.

We both know that's harder.

You need to try...don't you want to try to prevent it from happening to her?

NICOLE. No. I don't. I can't.

If you're asking if I'll try to not feed her french fries and cake, yeah, of course.

Just like you did.

If you're asking if I'll try and help her when Whit Russell comes to her in first grade and calls her fat ass, yeah of course.

You did that too.

If you're asking if I'll make her feel like no matter what, she'll never matter to me or to anyone else if she's fat... that there's some future version of herself that's thin and better and that's the "Real" her, I won't do that.

HELEN. But it IS possible. I did it, you can too –

NICOLE. Mom. I know you did it. But I'm not willing to do it like you are. I'm sorry. I'm not.

And honestly? Until Dad died and you had no husband or job or ANYTHING other than a diet, you weren't willing either.

NICOLE. I'm okay. And my maybe daughter will be okay too.

Even if she's fat.

Maybe even because of it.

Maybe someday she'll be like a motivational speaker for fat girls or something.

Maybe she'll be the first fat astronaut.

Or maybe she'll be unemployed and I'll scream at her for living in my basement.

I don't care. I will smile and LIE and say, "You're perfect!"

If you think that's dumb, I'm sorry.

HELEN. I don't think it's dumb.

I just think it's hard.

NICOLE. Well. I'll work at it. With all that extra energy I'll have from not fat shaming her.

HELEN. Well.

You sound like you have it all worked out.

I guess it'll be easy for you.

I'm sorry it wasn't for me.

> (**HELEN** *hands* **NICOLE** *the thing she got in her room. An old tape player with a tape inside.*)

You didn't give me any warning, so I don't have a real baby gift. But I thought this might be something you'd like.

I've been keeping it for myself for awhile.

But I think that might be selfish. So here.

Time to pass it on.

> (**NICOLE** *takes it.* **HELEN** *gathers up her things. She grabs her noodle.*)

It's almost time for rehearsal, so I'm off to the pool.

I guess you'll be gone when I get back.

I'm sorry this visit was less than pleasant.

I never understand how we got so wrong.

NICOLE. Of course you don't.

> (**ROBERT** *gives* **NICOLE** *an exasperated look.* **HELEN** *heads to the door, but gives* **ROBERT** *a tentative hug. She starts to exit. She gives* **NICOLE** *an awkward hug too.*)

HELEN. I do love you.

I know you think I don't. Or it's conditional. But I do.

> (**HELEN** *leaves space for* **NICOLE** *to say something.*)

> (**NICOLE** *looks at her, stonefaced. A long, long standoff.* **NICOLE** *will not bend.*)

> (*She won't say I love you.*)

> (*She won't say anything.*)

> (**HELEN** *eventually leaves. The screen door bangs. She's gone.*)

NICOLE. We're free!

> (**ROBERT** *doesn't say anything.*)

What?

ROBERT. (*Truly disappointed.*) Whewf. Man. You've got some of your Mom in you, despite what you might think... I'm gonna go finish packing the car.

> (*He gathers the backpack, and blow dryer, etc. He exits. A second or two later,* **AMY** *comes in with three large iced coffees. She's clearly just passed* **ROBERT**.)

AMY. Well, you're all up early. I was just gonna leave these in the fridge on my way to set up.

> (*She puts Robert's in the fridge and hands* **NICOLE** *one. She hangs onto her own, of course. There's a little pause as the two sip.*)

> (*Re:* **ROBERT,** *who seemed upset when she passed him offstage.*) He okay?

NICOLE. Eh. It's not gonna be a great car ride home.

> (*They sip again. After a moment...*)

AMY. Soooo. Are we not gonna, like, process last night?

NICOLE. There's nothing to process. Everything is exactly the same as it was. She's a narcissist who only cares about herself, so it's the same thesis as I've always had. And we're leaving because I'm an adult and I no longer have to ENGAGE with my family if I don't want to. So I packed the car and we are leaving directly from the shower.

AMY. That's fair.

NICOLE. I know.

AMY. But...Then you guys will just bury this like you always do, not talk for like two months, and then it'll be back to the same old thing. You'll never actually change it.

NICOLE. Well, unfortunately, it's not just up to me.

AMY. But one of you has to start. And last night! That was you starting. Someone has to try.

> (*Pause.*)

NICOLE. But can you believe the Down Syndrome thing though. "Down Syndrome children are lovely." Like actually? / That's insane.

AMY. / Batshit. Batshit.

(They both laugh. It is truly crazy.)

It's weird we're both gonna be Moms.

NICOLE. Right?

AMY. Our kids can be best friendsssssss! Eeeee!

NICOLE. God help *us.*

AMY. Totally.

(Pause.)

I just.

I wish I'd known beforehand. I would have gotten you something. I would have liked to know. I know we don't really talk when you aren't here. Like at all. But. I would have gotten you / a present, or something maybe.

NICOLE. *(Realizing.)* / Oh, Amy, I'm sorry. It's just. We weren't telling anyone yet.

Robert's actually so pissed I blurted it out like that. Especially to my mom. He says it's actually my way of being controlling. Rhonda will have a field day with that one!

(Longish pause.)

AMY. It's funny. I've known you since kindergarten. But sometimes I feel like there's this wall between us. I used to take it personally, but I guess more recently, I realized you do it to everyone. You're a bit of an arm's length kind of gal.

NICOLE. What? No I'm not.

AMY. You are. It's okay. I still love you.

NICOLE. I don't mean to be like that.

AMY. I know. Your Mom was kind of mean to you. It makes sense. You learned to not really get that close.

NICOLE. I feel close to you.

AMY. I'm glad.

NICOLE. I feel close to Robert.

AMY. I know. I like that.

> (*Pause.* **NICOLE** *rubs her tummy for the first time.*)

NICOLE. I want to be close to this baby. I'm scared I won't know how.

AMY. Everyone is scared of that. I'm scared I won't know how not to be an alcoholic because of my Mom. I'm scared I'll be depressed like my Dad. And I'm scared all of that will happen to *him* and I won't be able to stop it.

NICOLE. I can feel myself hardening like her.

I don't want to. But I don't know how to get out of it.

AMY. Just decide. Decide not to be like that.

That's what I'm doing.

NICOLE. You make it sound easy.

AMY. I have to, or you won't do it.

NICOLE. Fair.

AMY. It's nice.

We get to do it ourselves now. We get to try again.

Motherhood: the next generation.

And maybe it's a little better this time around?

NICOLE. Or maybe it's not.

> (**AMY** *shrugs.* **NICOLE**'s *eyes spy the tape deck.* **AMY** *sees it too.*)

AMY. What's that?

NICOLE. From my Mom. A baby gift, she said.

AMY. What is it?

NICOLE. It's probably a recording of her mantras about weight loss or something equally sinister.

AMY. It's probably a mix tape from 1981. Or wait...she hates pop music, doesn't she?

NICOLE. And jokes. And tattoos. And boats. And probably me.

AMY. That's the one thing she doesn't hate.

(**NICOLE** *looks down at her belly. The baby.*)

Well, hit play. Let's see what we've got. Rip off the band-aid.

NICOLE. Fiiiiine. LOOK I AM SOFTENING BEFORE YOUR EYES.

(**NICOLE** *plays the tape just as* **ROBERT** *renters.*)

ROBERT. Well, are we ready –

(*A guitar strums.**)

NICOLE. Oh my god...

(*Plays a little melody.*)

Oh god. I know what this is...

(**NICOLE** *almost immediately bursts into tears.*)

ROBERT. What? What is it?

NICOLE. When my parents...they used to work late at the bar. Emma had to watch me. I would have nightmares when they weren't home, I was scared of the dark –

---

* A license to produce *Nicole Clark Is Having a Baby* does not include a performance license for any third-party or copyrighted recordings. Licensees should create their own.

NICOLE'S FATHER'S VOICE. *(On the recording, broad, like a children's theater actor.)* Goldilocks and the Three Bears! ROAAAAR!

NICOLE. My Dad.

> *(**ROBERT** holds her. **AMY** takes her hand. Cute guitar music continues.)*

They recorded my favorite children's books. That's my mom...she plays by ear.

AMY. Oh yeah...that's right.

NICOLE. And my Dad...

NICOLE'S FATHER'S VOICE. *(On recording, narrating as a gruff bear.)* Once upon a time I was minding my own business in my cottage in the woods. It was me, Papa Bear. My wife, Mama Bear –

HELEN. *(On recording, as "Mama Bear.")* Oh hello!

NICOLE'S FATHER'S VOICE. And our son, Baby Bear.

HELEN. *(On recording as "Baby Bear.")* Waaah Waaahhh Mama! Papa!

BABY NICOLE. *(On recording as herself.)* Mama? Papa?

HELEN. *(On recording as herself.)* Yes, sweet girl...but we're bears! Bear Mama and Papa!

NICOLE'S FATHER'S VOICE. *(On recording as a bear.)* ROAAAAR!

> *(**BABY NICOLE** laughs and laughs. **HELEN** and **NICOLE'S FATHER** laugh too.)*

And on this particular morning, we all had a hankering for porridge--

> *(**NICOLE** lays her head down on the table as the recording continues with more of the story, her **DAD** narrating. She might be weeping.)*

NICOLE'S FATHER'S VOICE. *(On recording as gruff bear.)* So Mama Bear got to cooking.

HELEN. *(On recording as Mama Bear.)* Stir stir stir!

ROBERT. Are you okay?

NICOLE. I just miss her already.

> *(**AMY** and **ROBERT** hold **NICOLE**. They listen for a minute as the story plays on.)*

HELEN. *(On recording as Baby Bear.)* Mine mine mine! *(Then as Mama Bear.)* Not yet, Baby Bear. It's too hot. And I would NEVER let my Baby Bear get burned. Ouch!

> *(**BABY NICOLE** laughs.)*

> *(Lights fade on them there at the kitchen table.)*

Six Years Later...But Probably the Audience Doesn't Know It Yet

(**HELEN** *appears. Perhaps even while* **ROBERT,** **AMY,** *and* **NICOLE** *listen to the tape. We'll have to see. She's wearing her same bathrobe. But maybe she has a walker. Or her hair is different. Something we won't understand until we understand time has passed. I won't panic if that takes a beat or two.* **HELEN** *opens the fridge. It's night, so it just glows on her face. She stares at it for a long beat. She reaches for something. But changes her mind.*)

(*She closes the fridge. It's pretty dark. She makes her way over to the kitchen table, which perhaps takes her a bit more time than it did six years ago. She's had a hip replacement recently, so she's still on the mend. This will not be important. I'm just saying, things have happened. She still takes her swimming classes, though, don't worry. She's merely on hiatus.*)

(*She sits at the table and takes out her phone. She mindlessly scrolls. Quiet. After a beat or two,* **NICOLE** *comes in. Sees* **HELEN.** *Says nothing. She opens the fridge. She stares at it for a long beat. She reaches for something. But changes her mind.*)

(*She crosses to the table and sits. Perhaps she has grey roots now. Or different hair. Who knows? She reaches into her bathrobe pocket and takes out her phone.*)

(*Oh I forgot to mention that if the scenic budget allows and there's an elegant way to do it in the transition, it would be funny to add to the number of wolves* **HELEN** *has collected. One could do a lot of damage in six years of collecting wolves, after all.)*

(Back to the facts: the two women scroll and type and space out on their phones for a long while. If you do this correctly, it will be funny at some point. After a while **HELEN** *sighs in frustration. She starts shaking the phone like an etch-a-sketch (she's trying to get a video to be horizontal/full screen.). After a minute of this, she finally gives up and keeps it vertical. She hits play. We hear the something like the* Charles in Charge *theme song.* * *At the end* **NICOLE** *and* **HELEN** *both sing along with the recording, as if on autopilot...)*

HELEN. Oh you're speaking to me.

NICOLE. I wasn't speaking to you, I was singing WITH THE PHONE

HELEN. Now you're speaking to me.

NICOLE. Well NOW I am, just to clarify that I wasn't.

HELEN. Every time we're together, it's like you're sixteen years old.

NICOLE. I know and I hate it.

---

* A license to produce *Nicole Clark Is Having a Baby* does not include a performance license for the *Charles in Charge* theme song. The publisher and author suggest that the licensee contact ASCAP or BMI to ascertain the music publisher and contact such music publisher to license or acquire permission for performance of the song. If a license or permission is unattainable for the *Charles in Charge* theme song, the licensee may not use the song in *Nicole Clark Is Having a Baby* but should create an original composition in a similar style or use a similar song in the public domain. For further information, please see the Music and Third-Party Materials Use Note on page iii.

(Pause.)

HELEN. I'm sorry for what I said. I was just trying to be honest.

NICOLE. You know I hate birthdays I don't get her, so I don't know why you'd say it. Like what does it DO for you?

HELEN. I said I'm sorry! I was just trying to make sure you knew she'd be FINE without you!

NICOLE. WHAT A GIFT! THANK YOU!

HELEN. I don't know how many times I have to apologize.

NICOLE. You wouldn't have to apologize if it didn't HAPPEN.

HELEN. You know, no matter how old you get, you still don't seem to understand I'm just a PERSON. I make MISTAKES.

NICOLE. Oh please, I know you don't think that.

> (**HELEN** *says nothing. [She doesn't think that, by the way, she just knows she should think that.]* **NICOLE** *rolls her eyes.*)

HELEN. Well, since we're up, do you want some meat?

> (**NICOLE** *looks at her with daggers for eyes.*)

Geez, fine.

> *(A pause.)*

Are we just going to sit here in the dark?

NICOLE. You can go to bed.

HELEN. No. It's almost dawn, I won't sleep because I'll just be thinking it's too close to when I should get up.

NICOLE. *(Almost annoyed.)* That...happens to me too.

> (**NICOLE** *looks at her phone, an imaginary text she wishes she was getting.*)

HELEN. I really am sorry.

> (**NICOLE** *refreshes her phone.*)

I am!

NICOLE. It's just that you don't understand, you didn't have to do this. You didn't have to – and ugh fucking SHERYL gets to make her the carrot cake. It makes me nuts. You didn't have to lose me, ever.

HELEN. All mothers lose their daughters if they did a good enough job.

NICOLE. Have you been reading Elizabeth Gilbert again?

HELEN. Elizabeth Gilbert doesn't have children.

NICOLE. I know, that's why that's just the sort of basic bitch thing she would say.

> (**HELEN** *considers this. [Perhaps she did get that from Elizabeth Gilbert?]*)

HELEN. I'm just saying, all I'm saying is I haven't made you a birthday cake in years.

NICOLE. You didn't even make me a birthday cake when you could have made me a birthday cake.

HELEN. I was never much of a baker.

NICOLE. Too many calories.

HELEN. *(Trying to be cool and make a hilarious joke.)* PREACH! PREACH ABOUT IT! HAHAHA PREACH! PREACH! WERK! PREACH!

> (**NICOLE** *looks at* **HELEN** *like she's insane. Then* **NICOLE** *looks at her phone again.*)

Why don't you just call?

NICOLE. Too early. They won't be up yet.

HELEN. He'll have her call the minute she gets up. Robert is very thoughtful.

NICOLE. Hi, my name is Nicole and my mother wants me to shoot myself in the face.

HELEN. What?

NICOLE. CAN YOU NOT SIDE WITH MY EX RIGHT NOW YOU ACTUALLY HAVE NO IDEA IF HE IS THOUGHTFUL OR NOT

HELEN. He always seemed thoughtful.

NICOLE. Well, to many people I seem nice.

HELEN. *(Under her breath.)* Doubt it.

NICOLE. WHAT?

HELEN. Nothing. You sure you don't want any meat? Or I have hardboiled eggs. I did them fresh in the instant pot yesterday.

NICOLE. I'm fine.

> (**HELEN** *grimaces and stretches her leg/ hip.* **NICOLE** *gets up and gets an ice pack and hands it to her, then sits back down, refreshing the phone again.)*

HELEN. Are you gonna see Amy while you're here?

NICOLE. They don't get back from camping until Wednesday.

HELEN. You'll be gone by then.

NICOLE. *(An eye roll.)* Yes. I know.

HELEN. EVERYTHING I say is annoying, I get it.

NICOLE. I didn't say that.

HELEN. You didn't have to. I can read NONVERBAL cues, you know.

> (**NICOLE** *says nothing.)*

You don't have to punish me because you're upset. I didn't do it. I didn't make your custody arrangement.

NICOLE. I KNOW THAT.

HELEN. I'm trying to help! Why did you even come for a visit if all you were gonna do is be like this?

NICOLE. I THOUGHT IT WOULD HELP. I don't know WHY after all these years of it NEVER HELPING I thought... I don't know. I don't fucking know. I DON'T KNOW!

> (**NICOLE** *breaks down. But I'm not sure that means tears.* **HELEN** *reaches over, touches her, strokes her hair.*)

HELEN. Honey, I'm so sorry. I'm sorry you're in pain.

NICOLE. *(Weeping.)* I wanted to give her the Dora backpack! I'm the one who even knew she wanted it.

I know it's stupid

I hate that shit

I hate it

SHERYL

SHERYL IS SO NICE

SHERYL WEARS ROMPERS!!!

I kind of wish he HAD cheated on me with her, because I could have been like HOW

DID YOU EVEN GET HER CLOTHES OFF ROMPERS ARE IMPOSSIBLE

But noooo Robert is so thoughtful he never even cheated.

And now it BURNS ME she will think Robert and FUCKING SHERYL got her the Dora backpack

HELEN. They'll tell her it's from you, Robert *is* pretty thought –

NICOLE. *MOTHER.*

HELEN. Okay, right, okay.

NICOLE. Even if they tell her. She's six. She – it's. I don't get to see her put it on and wear it all day and fall asleep in it. I don't get to watch.

I HATE HIM

I HATE HIM EVEN THOUGH HE DIDN'T DO ANYTHING

I HATE HIM

She's mine.

She's mine.

She's mine.

> (**HELEN** *goes to touch or maybe hug* **NICOLE**, *but* **NICOLE** *stands up abruptly, not noticing.*)

I can't just sit here. This is making me crazy.

HELEN. It's too early to go to the pool! It's too early!

NICOLE. What? The pool? Why would we...?

HELEN. Oh I don't know I was just listing something.

Cards?

NICOLE. You hate games.

HELEN. I can pretend.

NICOLE. That's not fun.

HELEN. Garbage TV?

NICOLE. This early it's just like, the *300 Club*...

HELEN. The *700 Club*?

NICOLE. I never remember.

HELEN.　Me either. OH! OHHHHHH! Ooooo!!! What about! What about –

> (**HELEN** *races into the other room [but remember she may have a walker. Racing is... like it's still* **HELEN** *with a hip replacement racing.] So she like, run/hobbles/hops out.* **NICOLE** *stands there. She leans over and refreshes her phone again. Suddenly from the other room we hear music. It's a song in the style of Bonnie Raitt's "I Can't Make You Love Me."* * **HELEN** *enters hobbling, holding a boom box. She sings with it.)*

> (**HELEN** *sings the first few lines, then goes over to* **NICOLE**, *trying to get her to participate.* **NICOLE** *doesn't want to.* **HELEN** *sings a line or two more, but seeing* **NICOLE** *won't sing along, she steps away. She loses herself in the song and as she launches into the chorus, we learn...she actually has a good voice. She looks off into an imaginary audience. I think maybe* **HELEN** *always wanted to do this. Be a singer. Perform. Be seen. But she of course, like so so many, never could.)*

> (*After* **HELEN** *is fully in her zone,* **NICOLE** *joins in. The two sing together. Their voices blending. Somewhere here* **HELEN**, *perhaps for a moment, quiets her own singing a bit*

---

* A license to produce *Nicole Clark Is Having a Baby* does not include a performance license for Bonnie Raitt's "I Can't Make You Love Me." The publisher and author suggest that the licensee contact ASCAP or BMI to ascertain the music publisher and contact such music publisher to license or acquire permission for performance of the song. If a license or permission is unattainable for "I Can't Make You Love Me." the licensee may not use the song in *Nicole Clark Is Having a Baby* but should create an original composition in a similar style or use a similar song in the public domain. For further information, please see the Music and Third-Party Materials Use Note on page iii.

> *to listen to* **NICOLE**, *who, like her mother, has a truly beautiful voice. Or maybe it's just regular. But to each other, they are magic. As the chorus builds to a climactic point –.**)
>
> *(Nicole's phone rings. She immediately stops and runs to it and* **HELEN** *turns off the boom box.* **HELEN** *watches anxiously as* **NICOLE** *answers.)*

NICOLE & HELEN. *(Singing.*** **HELEN** *joins after* **NICOLE** *begins.)*
TODAY'S A SPECIAL DAY FOR YOU! JUST FOR YOU
TODAY'S A SPECIAL DAY FOR YOU! JUST FOR YOU-OO
YOU ARE ONE YEAR OLDER! WHOOPTY DOOPTY DOO!
HAPPY BIRTHDAY JUST FOR YOU! WHOOPTY DO!

HELEN. *(Interjecting.)* Hi Maya! It's Glammy!

NICOLE. I heard! I know!

Woowwwww! Dora, huh? ....

> *(***HELEN** *smiles,* **NICOLE** *smiles at her.)*

Pink?!?! No way. No way.

What did you have –

Waffles?

PRINCESS PANCAKES?

---

* Under no circumstances is this to be played as a secret message to each other, or as a huge subtextual moment where they are saying what they could never say through song. They are literally just singing a song they both used to sing when **NICOLE** was young. They are enjoying the technical act of singing a song. Please don't overplay this. Let the actors sing it and love it. That's all.

** A license to produce *Nicole Clark Is Having a Baby* does not include a performance license for any third-party or copyrighted music. Licensees should create an original composition or use music in the public domain. For further information, please see the Music and Third-Party Materials Use Note on page iii.

Wow! Daddy must be –

> (**HELEN** *settles in the chair next to* **NICOLE** *to listen.*)

Carrot cake, of course.

Oh, cream cheese frosting?

Shirley Temple! You're so fancy! GIRL!

Did Daddy make the cupcakes for your class?

No, it's okay, I'll ask him later...

He did!

Gushers?!

Those are so bad for you!

I guess it's only one day. Only one day you can be bad...

No, honey not BAD just.

Nevermind.

Tell me what else you're – is Bella going with you guys or...

Oh, Iris huh?

> (*She eyes* **HELEN**, *juicy gossip! Bella got demoted!*)

I didn't know.

Ooo! That sounds so fun, honey. You're a little fashionista!

...I love you so much.

> (**NICOLE** *starts to cry, but her voice doesn't change.* **HELEN** *inches closer. She wraps her arms around her.*)

NICOLE. I can't wait to see you very soon. Three more sleeps.

And then we can celebrate. Ladies on the TOWN!

Of course we are! Yes!

Anything you want...maybe even till ten-thirty!

I miss you, too, sweetie.

I miss you so so so so much.

> (**HELEN** *kisses* **NICOLE***'s head as she holds her.* **NICOLE** *laughs at something Maya has said. She's about to say something else when suddenly –.)*

> (*Blackout.*)

End of Play